# TRUE CONFESSION

"Oh, dear!" Helena exclaimed. "I didn't remember until you said what you just did! A night or two before Harry took off for the Circle Star, he'd been hitting the bottle a mite too much. Maybe I had, too, because I'm just remembering what he said. . . ."

Ki waited for her to go on, but Helena had covered her mouth with her hand and was staring fixedly ahead.

"What did he say?" Ki asked. "Tell me!"

"That he'd take care of things so we'd never have to worry about money or going to jail again. And you know what that means as well as I do. He don't intend for you or Jessie Starbuck to get out of this alive!"

WESLEY ELLIS

# LONE STAR

## AND THE
## RENEGADE RANGER

JOVE BOOKS, NEW YORK

LONE STAR AND THE RENEGADE RANGER

A Jove Book/published by arrangement with
the author

PRINTING HISTORY
Jove edition/April 1990

ISBN: 0-515-10287-3

Jove Books are published by The Berkley Publishing Group,
200 Madison Avenue, New York, New York 10016. The name
''Jove'' and the ''J'' logo are trademarks belonging
to Jove Publications, Inc.

PRINTED IN THE UNITED STATES OF AMERICA

10  9  8  7  6  5  4  3  2  1

# Chapter 1

"Are you satisfied now that I knew nothing of this, Don Arturo?" Jessie asked. With her thumb she riffled the small stack of ledger sheets that the man across the desk had been examining and had now returned to her. "As you've seen, these reports and statements that the manager of my mine in Silver City has sent me show that all the taxes due to New Mexico Territory have been paid."

"Very true, Miss Starbuck," Don Arturo replied. "But the records here in my office do not show that the sums itemized on your reports have been received."

Jessie glanced at Ki, who sat beside her in the office of Don Arturo de Vega y Lopez, the treasurer of New Mexico Territory. Ki indicated the ledger sheets that were scattered across the desk between them and the territory's chief tax collector and nodded. No words were needed between him and Jessie; they'd already discussed the problem that had brought them to the territorial capital.

1

"I'm sure your office records are correct," Jessie said. "Unless . . ." She let her voice trail off as a thoughtful frown formed on her face.

"Unless one of our clerks has been stealing them?"

"I didn't like to suggest that," Jessie replied.

"Of course. But the same thought occurred to me. I'm sure you understand that Santa Fe is a small town, and New Mexico Territory has few banks. I have investigated the two people in my office who are the only ones in positions which would allow them to embezzle. I'm satisfied that they have not done so."

"Then I'd say it's pretty obvious that the manager of my mine must be stealing from me," Jessie said with a frown.

"That thought has occurred to me as well," Don Arturo went on. "If I may be blunt, he has been stealing from you by falsifying the financial reports he sent us to show that no taxes were due. He sent you the true figures, of course, showing as taxes the money he pocketed. I'm sure you know it is a manner of stealing that we politely call embezzling."

"I don't believe in being polite in a case of this sort," Jessie said. "Theft, stealing, robbing—any of those words describes the situation much more accurately."

"Thefts carried out in this manner are not new to those of us who serve in the territory's Treasury Department. I see it far too often in my job as the territorial treasurer," Don Arturo said. "And I regret that you have been forced to make such a long and tiring trip. I'm sure that since you now know the situation, you will take steps to correct it?"

"Of course. Ki and I will go to Silver City at once and find out about the mine's true financial situation.

As soon as I know that, I'll make whatever arrangements are necessary to pay the arrears."

Ki had been silent during the conversation between Jessie and the official. Now he asked, "Aren't you forgetting the roundup, Jessie? All the arrangements have been made for it."

Jessie smiled a bit ruefully. "You're right, Ki," she said. Turning back to Don Arturo, she went on, "You're familiar with ranch life, I suppose, Don Arturo?"

"But of course!" the official replied. "In fact, my father, whose name I bear in turn as a family custom, visited your famous Circle Star Ranch once while your esteemed father was completing its formation. Our family ranch has benefitted by many of the things your father showed him."

"I didn't realize that you are a rancher as well as the territory's treasury secretary," Jessie said. She was standing up as she spoke, and Ki was following her example. She went on, "When you find time, you must come and visit us."

"To be truthful, I enjoy the ranch more than I do this office," Don Arturo said with a smile. "And do not worry about this stir over your mine's delinquent taxes, Miss Starbuck. I called it to your attention in my letter only because I am required by law to do so."

"Of course." Jessie nodded. "But Ki and I will go to the mine as soon as we finish our roundup on the Circle Star. I'm anxious to get things straightened out there."

As Ki and Jessie picked their way along the crowded *portal* where the usual crowd of Indians from the nearby pueblos were gathered, displaying

3

the tribal artifacts they offered for sale, she turned to Ki and shook her head.

"There are a lot of things about Santa Fe that've always fascinated me," she said as they crossed the street and started angling across the busy plaza toward La Fonda Hotel. "And this is one of them. Can you imagine the officials in any other state letting jewelry and crockery be sold at the entrance to the capitol?"

"Only in Santa Fe," Ki smiled.

"Yes," Jessie agreed. "And now that we've finished our business here so much quicker than we'd expected to, if it wasn't for the roundup, I'd like nothing better than to stay a few days and just enjoy poking around."

"I'm sure we'd both enjoy it," Ki agreed.

Jessie went on, "But with the cattle cars ordered to ship out the market herd as soon as the steers are cut out, and a trip to Silver City as soon as that's done, it's just not possible to stay."

"We'll have to hurry our packing if we intend to get the hotel stage to Lamy," Ki suggested. They were within a few steps of the massive earth-brown bulk of La Fonda now. "We'd better stop at the desk when we get inside and tell them we'll be taking the hotel's stage to Lamy."

They crossed the cavernous lobby, Jessie's boot-heels ringing on the floor of ornate Moorish tiles, and stopped at the registration desk.

"Señorita Starbuck, Señor Ki," the desk clerk said, nodding. "You wish your room keys, no?"

"Yes," Jessie replied. "And we'll be checking out as soon as we've packed, so please reserve us two seats on the next stage to Lamy."

"I am afraid that will not be possible, Señorita

4

Starbuck," the clerk said with a frown. "The Santa Fe Railroad agent has just left, he notified us that there has been a serious wreck on the line at Raton Pass, and no trains will run for three, perhaps four days."

Jessie and Ki exchanged glances. Ki said, "It looks like we're going to extend our visit here whether we want to or not."

"We can't afford to lose three or four days here, Ki. Not with the hands at the Circle Star expecting us for the roundup." Jessie frowned.

"Yes, I can see that," Ki said. "But we certainly can't go all the way to the Circle Star on horseback."

"Of course not. But we can't wait here a week, perhaps longer. Oh, how I wish I had Sun here now!"

"Perhaps the wreck isn't as bad as it's been reported," Ki said. "We certainly can't walk to Albuquerque."

"No," Jessie replied thoughtfully. "But we can go to Albuquerque on horseback. I'm sure the trains will be running west from there." Turning back to the clerk, Jessie went on, "You do have horses to rent, as I remember."

"Of course, Señorita Starbuck," the clerk said. "As well as the saddle gear you will need, of course. And since you are going to Albuquerque, you can leave them at Mr. Harvey's hotel there."

For a moment Ki was silent, then he said thoughtfully, "I can see where we'd save a lot of time. But it'd be a long ride."

"I don't mind it a bit," Jessie told him. "In fact, I think I'd enjoy riding a horse more than I would sitting in a hard seat on a stuffy train. Let's do it!"

• • •

"You know, Ki," Jessie said, "I don't want to sound cruel and heartless, but I'm almost glad there was a wreck on the railroad line. This is beautiful country, and we've never seen it before."

Jessie had been gazing for the past several minutes across the sparse growth of stunted *piñon* trees that stretched away from the narrow winding gravel-studded road. She turned in her saddle to face Ki.

"There's something about the restful atmosphere in Santa Fe that a railroad might ruin," she went on. "Bringing in a lot of people and perhaps turning it into a city, the way Albuquerque's grown. Why, there's nothing much left of the old Albuquerque anymore."

"Yes, I noticed that myself when we passed through it on the way to Santa Fe," Ki agreed. "The old part of town's falling into ruins, and there's an entirely new town clumping up around the depot."

Before Jessie could reply, a rifle cracked from one of the clumps of *piñons* that studded the slope ahead of them. Both she and Ki froze in their saddles as the bullet whistled between them and thunked into the dry hard yellow soil of the slope they'd just left. Then they moved swiftly, with quick precision, their reflexes honed to a razor edge by the years they'd spent fighting the sinister European cabal whose gunmen had murdered Jessie's father when he refused to join in its attempts to loot the natural riches of America.

Reining their horses off the road, Jessie and Ki were still spurring to the cover of the nearest cluster of low-growing trees when a second shot followed. It was no more accurate than the first had been. It went high and whistled to a thudding stop in the trunk of one of the *piñon* trees beside the road. The tree

6

was a scant foot from Jessie's horse, and she began reining the animal from side to side in short zigzags as they rode deeper into the scant cover the straggled cluster of *piñons* provided.

"Did you see where either of those shots came from?" Jessie asked as they pulled up and dismounted, then began scanning the landscape through the tree branches. Jessie had drawn her Colt as they turned off the narrow trace, and as she spoke she kept her eyes busy examining the upslope ahead.

Ki shook his head. "All I'm sure of is that whoever did the shooting is somewhere in front of us. I was too busy looking for cover to see where the muzzle-blast showed."

"So was I," Jessie said.

Almost before she'd finished speaking, a third shot broke the late afternoon stillness. A small spurt of yellowish dust kicked up from the hard stretch of soil between the trail and the tree clump where they'd taken cover. This time they could see the quickly dissolving puff of gunsmoke rising into the quiet air. It hung briefly above a cluster of trees on the long slope ahead, but though the trees were small and sparsely branched, they could see no movement that would give them a target.

Jessie let off a quick shot into the stand of trees. They heard the slug thunk into one of the tree trunks. A replying shot broke the air. The slug fell short and kicked up dust at the edge of the trace. A thin wisp of yellowish gunsmoke was dissipating above the foliage that shielded their ambushers.

Jessie did not reply with another shot. She saved her shells until she could see a definite target. Turning to Ki, she said with a puzzled frown, "I don't see how or why there'd be anybody after us, Ki. It's been a long while since we were in New Mexico Territory."

"We can't be sure they're after us in particular," Ki pointed out.

Jessie was still following her original train of thought. She went on, "We didn't notice anyone following us out of Santa Fe. I'm sure if there'd been somebody following us, we'd have noticed them along that wide stretch of flatland we crossed while we were riding along the riverbank before we started up these little mountains."

"No, there wasn't anyone following us," Ki agreed. "You're right, we'd have been sure to see them."

"Then that means whoever's after us is probably a local outlaw, or maybe two of them, who saw us coming along the trail and decided to ambush us and rob us."

Ki did not reply at once. He'd dropped from his saddle as the sharp barking of the last short broke the stillness and the bullet whistled past uncomfortably close to him. If the near-miss bothered him, Ki did not show it.

"That's my guess, too, Jessie," he told her. "It might be a pair of outlaws traveling together. I can't be sure, but one of those rifle shots sounded different from the other two."

"I was too busy looking for cover to notice anything like that," Jessie said. She was dismounting now. Stepping up to Ki's position, she hunkered down beside him. "But right now, I wish I'd brought my rifle along instead of leaving it at the Circle Star."

"And while we're wishing, I'd like to've glimpsed some muzzle blast or powder smoke," Ki replied. "In this kind of country, where there's so little vegetation, it's not always easy to spot a sniper's hiding place. But there's plenty of cover for me to make a *ninja* advance. I could easily get close enough to use my *shuriken*."

"I don't like feeling helpless," Jessie said, frowning. "And unless we start fighting back, those snipers are going to be inching up on us pretty soon."

"They haven't fired a shot for several minutes. They might be moving toward us now."

"Let me get a handful of shells out of my saddlebag," Jessie said. "Then we'll split up. You slant off to the right, I'll go to the left, and we'll get them pinned down between us."

"Fine," Ki said. He was examining the terrain between their position in the little grove of trees and the area from which the shots had come. "As nearly as I can tell, they're in that tallest stand of trees, on the other side of the trail, up the slope. Give me a start and I'll circle around them."

Jessie had been studying the slope that rose in front of them. She said, "Just be careful not to go up the slope beyond them, Ki. Stay to your right. I'll be moving directly toward them, and you won't be in danger of getting in line with one of my shots if you keep on my right side."

Ki frowned. "They haven't shot for several minutes. They might be moving, too."

"It's not likely they'll be moving fast with the groundcover as thin as it is," Jessie said. "We should be able to spot them as soon as we get out of this little stand of trees."

Jessie turned to watch Ki as he started out. He acknowledged her words with a nod over his shoulder as he kept moving slowly in the direction he'd chosen to take.

For a moment Jessie kept her eyes on Ki, then turned her attention to the landscape beyond his starting point. She studied the area where he was heading and fixed in her memory the location of the half-dozen *piñon* stands where Ki would be taking cover. After she was certain that she would not make the mistake of firing a shot into a clump of trees that were concealing Ki, she began her own advance.

Ki disappeared very quickly. In his dark-colored trousers and loosely fitted blouse he'd already used his *ninja* skill to merge into the mottled landscape. As she turned her eyes to the slope ahead, she glimpsed the darting reflection of the sun's rays when they were caught on the polished blued steel of a rifle barrel. Bringing up her Colt, she hugged the slender trunk of the tree she stood beside, and waited for a more certain target.

Her wait was not a long one. The almost noiseless brushing of Ki's footsteps had barely died away when once again on the upslope ahead she saw the unmistakable glistening of sunshine reflected from blued steel. Taking no chances of a hasty snapshot this time, Jessie crooked her elbow and with her left hand grasped the trunk of the small scrubby tree that was her only cover.

Gripping the trunk of the tree with her left hand, she used her arm as a rest for the hand in which she held her revolver and sighted along the barrel of the Colt. She saw at once that it was long range for a pistol, but made a quick estimate of the distance to her skimpy target and elevated the barrel. She waited as the distant rifle barrel was lowered and the forearm and shoulder of the man holding it came into sight. The moment the rifleman's head appeared when he leaned out to sight, she triggered the Colt.

A yell of pain sounded and the distant marksman let his rifle clatter to the ground. Jessie did not move when a second rifle barked from a point a score of yards to one side of the wounded sniper and the bullet kicked up a spurt of ocher earth as it plowed into the ground two or three paces from her position.

From some point invisible to her and beyond the man she was watching, still another rifle cracked, and its blast was echoed by yet another shot. Before the echoes of the second shot had died away, it was followed by two shots in quick succession and from an entirely different direction. These were both pistol shots, and Jessie frowned, for as yet none of the men who'd fired at her and Ki had fired anything except rifles.

Then a man's voice rose in a shout, *"Rendicen! Rendicen inmediatemente o matarte!"*

Jessie's smattering of Spanish was enough to allow her to translate the command for the men who'd attacked her and Ki to surrender or be killed, but she was unable to imagine who might have shouted the order. She was scanning the slope ahead as best she could without breaking cover when another sharp shout of pain broke the silence. Though the man who'd cried out was still unseen, there was pain in his voice as he replied.

*"Cedemos!"* he yelled. *"En el nombre de Dios, no matenos!"*

*"Bueno! Ponen sus fusiles a la tierra, y viente aca con sus brazos en el aire!,"* replied the man who'd given the order for the concealed snipers to drop their weapons and surrender.

Unwilling at the moment to do anything other than listen, Jessie held her position. She could hear the voices of several men talking in rapid-fire Spanish,

11

but they were too far away for her to make out more than an occasional mumbled word or two.

For a few seconds she considered calling to Ki, then a quick cautious second thought led her to delay showing herself or causing Ki to leave whatever shelter he'd found until she could be sure the exchange of shots and shouts was not a ruse designed to bring them out of the places where they'd taken cover. She did not call to him, but stood engaged in her silent debate until Ki's raised voice reached her.

"Jessie!" he shouted. "It's all right! Come join us!"

Ki's assurance was all that Jessie needed. She untied the reins of her horse and led the animal through the trees until she reached the trail. On the winding path ahead she could see Ki and a man strange to her moving around three other men, who stood with their arms raised above their heads.

As she drew closer and passed the last clump of trees that had obstructed her view, she saw a fifth man approaching the group on the trail from a distance in the opposite direction. From some still-invisible spot beyond him she could hear the faint bleating of sheep, and by the time she'd reached the group, she could also hear the grating of the animals' hooves on the graveled soil.

"This gentleman who's been helping us is Mr. Elfegeo Baca, Jessie," Ki said. "I've just been trying to thank him for stopping to give us a hand. Mr. Baca, let me present Miss Jessica Starbuck."

★

# Chapter 2

"I'll certainly add my thanks to Ki's," Jessie said, extending her hand.

While they shook hands, Jessie was taking stock of the man who'd come to their assistance. Elfegeo Baca appeared to be in his early twenties. His high cheekbones were tanned, his eyes dark under sparse narrow brows. His nose was prominent, but neither craggy nor unduly large, though his rather thin face gave its straight bridge and thick nostrils the appearance of dominating his features. He'd pushed his wide-brimmed hat back on his head; a few strands of dark brown hair stuck out below it and straggled across his high forehead. His chin was narrow with an upturned knobby point.

"It was nothing," Baca said with a shrug after he'd taken Jessie's hand briefly and bowed over it. "A part of my job. In my home in Socorro County, beyond Albuquerque, I am a deputy to the sheriff, and I did only what anyone else in my position would have done."

"Well, it was both brave and thoughtful," Jessie said. "We certainly weren't expecting to be waylaid, especially so close to town, or we'd have been better prepared."

"I see you have a revolver," Baca went on. "Unless you have objections, will you hold it on my prisoners for a moment, Miss Starbuck? I will need both hands to tie their wrists with the rope my nephew is bringing. And if you see a need to shoot, do not hesitate to do so."

"You're arresting them, then?" Jessie asked.

"*De verdad*," Baca said, nodding. "Of course I arrest them. I know them, all three." Pointing as he spoke, he went on, "That is Juan Griego. He is out of jail on bond for stealing. The one next to him is Trano Salezar, and I have arrested him for theft before now. The one with the blood on his arm is Carlos Huerta, a no-good from Tijeras. We have also become acquainted earlier."

"I know you have little regard for the men you shoot," Huerta grunted. "Or you would by now have taken care of binding up the wound you made in my arm."

"*Callate!*" Baca growled. "I looked at the scratch on your arm, Huerta. It no longer bleeds. You need no bandage."

"If I can—" Jessie began, but broke off when gravel grated on the trail that rose ahead of them and a younger version of Elfegeo Baca came skidding down the incline carrying a looped rope.

"Here you are, Tío Fegeo," he said, tossing Baca the coil. "Or do you want me to tie them for you?"

"I tie my own prisoners, you know that!" Baca grunted. "Some day I will buy two or three more pairs of handcuffs and will not need rope any longer.

14

Here. Take my pistol and help Miss Starbuck to cover them while I see to these *ladrones*." As an afterthought he turned back to Jessie and Ki and went on, "My nephew, Ramon Sandoval. Now, you will please excuse me while I fix these scoundrels so they can do no more harm."

As Jessie and the newcomer shook hands, she realized that she was looking at a younger and strikingly handsome version of Elfegeo Baca. Ramon's shoulders were broad, and she could see the flexing of sturdy muscles under the taut fabric of his jeans and shirtsleeves. He looked a great deal like a younger version of his uncle, and Jessie imagined that he might at some time in the future begin to emulate the older man.

"Your resemblance to your uncle is striking," she remarked.

He nodded. "It is that way in our family. But Tío Fegeo is the strong one. He sees that we uphold the family name, as well as our resemblance to each other."

"Enough, now!" Baca said. "We have work to do and a long way left to travel. The day is already dying."

Leaving Jessie and Ki and young Sandoval to guard the three prisoners while he worked, Baca lashed the outlaws' wrists, leaving them connected by a length of the rope. He finished the job quickly and efficiently, then turned back to the others.

"If I did not have a duty to perform and a promise to Ramon to keep, I would turn back and go with you and your friend to Albuquerque, to be sure you arrive there safely. These men are not the only outlaws who roam the hills around us."

"Oh, Ki and I can take care of ourselves quite well, Mr. Baca," Jessie said quickly. "And we un-

15

derstand that you have a duty to take care of your prisoners. We're very grateful to you for your help, but please don't worry about us."

"I don't suppose there's a town closer to us, where you could leave your prisoners in jail while you're driving your sheep to whatever it is you're taking them?" Ki asked.

"There are no jails closer than Albuquerque or Santa Fe, and we are almost exactly between the two," Baca replied. "The small villages and the Indian pueblos that are closer to this place do not have jails. But there are better reasons for taking the prisoners with us. I am helping my nephew drive his sheep to Pojoaque, and it is north of Santa Fe. It will be no trouble to take these outlaws with us and put them in the prison in Santa Fe, then we will travel on with the sheep."

Jessie frowned. "With this delay, you don't expect to get even as far as Santa Fe this evening, do you?"

"Most certainly not," Baca answered, flicking his hand toward the declining sun. "If we—" He stopped, frowned, and went on, "Are you and your companion in a great hurry to reach Albuquerque, Miss Starbuck?"

"We're going there to board the first train that will get us to my ranch in Texas," Jessie explained. "It's in the Big Bend country, not an easy part of Texas to reach from here."

"Then you and your companion would be in no more of a hurry than Ramon and I," Baca said.

"Probably not," Jessie replied. "But what difference does that make?"

"As our saying here goes, "*como si, como sa*,"" Baca said. "There is a small creek that forms a pond only a short distance from here. Perhaps it would be

16

wise for all of us to stop beside it. I will feel better if I am sure that you and your companion are safe tonight."

"Ki and I are used to stopping wherever darkness catches us, Mr. Baca," Jessie protested. "And stopping to help us has already taken up a lot of your time when you should've been traveling."

"That's of small importance," Baca assured her. "We must stop whether we wish to or not. Sheep cannot be driven at night, and they must be watered as well."

Jessie and Ki exchanged glances, then nodded almost imperceptibly. Turning to face Baca again, Jessie said, "If you're sure you won't mind stopping earlier than I'm sure you'd planned to, we'll take your very thoughtful suggestion."

"Very good," he said. "If you do not object to a small walk, Ramon and I will load these outlaws on your horses, then I will lead you to where you can see the small pond I have mentioned. Then perhaps you and your companion will be able to kindle a small fire and at the same time keep an eye on my prisoners. I will go back with Ramon to drive the sheep to the pond."

"I'll start back to the sheep," Ramon volunteered. "By the time you come to join me, I will have them ready to move."

Leading their horses, the outlaws lying across the animals' backs like three sacks of meal, Jessie and Ki walked beside Elfegeo Baca as he started away from the trail. He led them toward a low ragged ridge that broke the western skyline. Except for the occasional small stands of low-growing *piñon* trees and a few patches of weedy vines, the ridge was barren. There was no sign of a trail, but Baca led the way without hesitation to the ridge and up its slope.

They reached its crest, and Jessie exclaimed with delight when she saw the small oval depression that was revealed below. In its spoon-shaped hollow there were waist-high and shoulder-high pine trees growing from a carpet of low grass around the bank of a small purling creek that at the bottom of the hollow spread to form a little pond. The rays of the low-dropping sun danced gently on the water's lucent blue surface.

"This will be a lovely place to spend the night," she said. "I'd begun to think we weren't going to find anything but bare ground where we could stop."

"There are few places like it in these barren mountains," Baca agreed. "And fewer people who know where to find them." He gestured toward the horses and the men lashed across their backs. "If you tie these *ladrones* to the base of sturdy trees, they will give you no trouble."

"Ki and I have had enough experience with their kind to know how to handle them," Jessie volunteered. "Don't worry about us. And we'll start a fire, too."

"I'll leave you here, then," Baca said. "It is no great distance to the sheep herd. Ramon and I will have the animals here by the time you tie these outlaws to tree trunks and get a small fire started."

As they watched Baca ride off and disappear in the broken country that led to the main trail, Jessie turned to Ki. "A very unusual man, Mr. Baca. Luck was on our side when he heard those outlaws shooting at us and came to help us."

"Yes," Ki agreed. "He seems to be a somewhat remarkable man in more ways than one."

"Let's do our chores, then," Jessie went on. "It'll

18

be dark soon, and we've got more than enough to do to keep us busy."

"We'd better attend to Mr. Baca's prisoners first," Ki suggested.

Jessie glanced at their surroundings and indicated a clump of aspens a little distance away. "Those seem to be the sturdiest trees in sight," she suggested. "It's not very close to our camp, but I don't see any trees closer that are big enough to hold them."

"You're right," Ki agreed after a quick glance around. "Let's get them secure, then we'll rest until Mr. Baca and his nephew come back."

Leaving Jessie to hold her Colt on the captives, Ki lashed the silently sullen prisoners, each man to his own tree. As a final precaution, he connected them by looping the rope's end over their shoulders after taking a turn of it around the necks of each man. He finished the job quickly and efficiently, then turned back to Jessie.

"Shall we go spread our bedrolls while we wait for Mr. Baca and his nephew to get back?" he asked.

"It's the best place I can think of," Jessie replied. "And we'll put out what food we brought along. After all this unexpected activity, I'm as hungry as a bear!"

"Do you think we should take turns standing watch tonight?" Jessie asked Elfegeo Baca, looking at him across the waning blaze of their small campfire. "Ki and I are accustomed to taking our turns at night herd when we're out on the range with the ranch hands at home."

Baca shook his head. "I wake to the smallest noise, Miss Starbuck, and I've taught Ramon to be alert.

If the prisoners try to get away, one of us will be sure to hear them."

"Besides that, they know that Tío Fegeo is about the quickest and best man with a gun in the territory," Ramon said quickly. "No outlaw with any sense will give him trouble. Why, it was from Billy the Kid himself that Tío Fegeo learned to shoot with a revolver."

"Be quiet, now!" Baca admonished his nephew. "Miss Starbuck and Ki are not interested in such things! Besides, that was several years ago. I have better sense now."

"I'm sure you know much more than we do about how our prisoners will behave," Ki put in quickly.

"Perhaps I do," Baca said with a smile. "These outlaws know they will suffer if they try to escape, and I have learned to sleep very lightly, with an ear always open. We have nothing to worry about. They will behave."

Around the dying embers of the fire which Ramon had kindled when he and his uncle returned with the small herd of sheep, Jessie and Ki sat on the large flat stones that Ramon had insisted on lugging up before they ate supper. Elfegeo Baca and the younger man lounged stretched out on the thinly grassed ground, propped up on their elbows.

Separated as they were by a space of twenty or thirty feet from their captors, the three prisoners were making the best of their situation in silence, the wrists of two of them tied and the third hand-cuffed to the trunks of the small pine trees that dotted the valley floor.

Though there was no moon, countless stars twin-kling through the thin clear night air of the mile-high altitude made the star-studded sky seem only a little darker than it had been in the hour before sundown. The occasional nasal blatting of a sheep that broke the quiet of the small oval valley seemed to be as much a part of the night as did the gentle rustle of the stunted fir trees in the capricious breeze.

"Then if there's no reason to stand watch, I think I'll go to bed," Jessie told her companions. "We still have quite a long way to travel tomorrow."

"But the road is easy, even if it is all uphill," Baca said. "There are only two small streams to cross, and they will give you no trouble."

While Jessie and Baca were talking, Ki had gotten up and stepped over to the pile of saddles and gear that lay a few steps away from the fire. He freed Jessie's blankets and his own from their lashings and walked back to the fire. As he approached Jessie he saw Baca leaving, starting toward the prisoners to check on them.

"I'll let you choose your own place to bed down, Jessie," Ki said. "I'll spread my bedroll fairly close to the horses, in case they get restless during the night."

"I'm as sure they're as ready to rest as we are, Ki," she replied. "And that patch of grass under the little pine tree over there looks good to me, though I'm sure that none of us will need any lullabies to put us to sleep."

Within the space of the next few minutes all of them had settled into their bedrolls and the impromptu camp was silent except for an occasional whinney from one of the tethered horses.

Jessie had no idea how long she'd been sleeping when the metallic clinking of metal on metal brought her wide awake. She sat up in her blankets, her ears straining as she tried to discover the source of the noise that had aroused her. After a moment she heard the metallic tinkle again, and the realization that the clinking had come from the steel links in the short chains that joined the handcuffs of the outlaw that Elfegeo Baca had shackled brought her sitting upright in her bedroll.

When the sound was repeated, Jessie decided to investigate, if only to satisfy herself that the noise was harmless. She thought of wakening Ki or Elfegeo Baca, but decided instantly that noiselessness and speedy action were more important. Reaching for the butt of her Colt, she sat up and slipped from her bedroll. As she started to step into her boots she realized that their crunching on the dry stone-studded soil would alert the prisoners if they were indeed trying to escape their fetters. Abandoning the idea, she levered herself to her feet and started toward the small stand of trees where Baca had placed the handcuffed men.

Though Jessie moved as silently as possible, each time she put her weight on her carefully advanced foot the dry rocky soil made a small crunching noise. She stopped after she'd taken only a half-dozen steps and listened. She discounted the occasional distant bleat from the sheep and the clicking sounds of their small sharp feet, which were the only sounds that broke the night now.

While she'd slept, the moon had started rising. Against the deep midnight blue of the sky, she could see the serrated horizon line, but though she scanned it carefully, there was no silhouetted moving form outlined against it. Standing poised and ready to move, Jessie studied the three dark rectangles marking the places where her companions had spread their bedrolls.

There was no movement visible in any of them. Her eyes had adjusted to the darkness by now, and Jessie stared into the darkness, trying to locate the cluster of trees where the prisoners were secured, but clumps of high brush hid the place. Moving cautiously, planting her feet straight down and settling her weight carefully on the foot she'd advanced, Jessie started toward the brush clump. She was halfway to her objective when a small noise of leaves and branches rustling reached her ears.

Jessie was only a step or two from the brushy patch where she'd heard the rustling. She stopped to listen again, but no more noises from the direction of the outlaws reached her ears. Then the brush rustled once more.

Unhesitatingly now, Jessie moved in the direction of the sound. She was within a yard of the sprawled growth of head-high *piñon* saplings when she stopped to listen again. The silence remained unbroken, and she was debating whether to push through the edges of the patch at the risk of making a noise when Ramon's whisper-pitched voice reached her.

"Don't be alarmed, Miss Starbuck. It's only me. I was sure I heard the outlaw's handcuffs clinking, so I went to look at them."

"You've already looked at them, then?"

"Yes. I tested their ropes; they are all secure."

"That must have been the clinking noise I heard, then, made by the man who's handcuffed."

"Yes. I'm sorry if I disturbed you."

"You didn't," Jessie replied. "But hearing that noise made me think the prisoners might be trying to escape."

"Then you should've called Tío Fegeo or me," Ramon said.

"I'm used to doing things for myself," she told him. "As I can see that you are, too."

"I only did what I was taught to do by my father and by Tío Fegeo. But a lady should not be expected to take the same risks which men do."

"I took very little risk," Jessie said, smiling. She lifted her hand to show Ramon the Colt, which had been hidden by the folds of her short riding skirt. "Didn't you bring your revolver, too?"

"I do not own a pistol," Ramon admitted. "A rifle can be used for hunting, but a pistol is only good for killing. And you handle your gun very much as Tío Fegeo does, as though you have used it often."

"My father gave me this Colt and taught me to use it," Jessie told him. Her voice was suddenly very sober. "That was at a time when he was at great risk. He knew I shared the risk only because I was his daughter."

"He was a wise man, then."

"Yes. And he was a gentle man as well, though when he needed to be he could be very hard indeed."

Ramon frowned. "You say he 'was.' He is dead, then?"

Jessie nodded. "Killed by enemies who wanted him to turn against his own country."

"They were traitors, then, who killed him?"

"Rich traitors," Jessie replied. "Rich, but always greedy for more. They wanted my father to help them destroy his country, using the wealth he'd earned by his hard work."

"How did your father become rich? When I see the *ricos* whose families came here as *conquistadores* and who own great tracts of land and have all they

24

wish, I have wondered how they are different from the rest of us."

"Perhaps they started just as you are, or as my father did, with very little but their ability to make great things from little ones."

"This is what your father did?" When Jessie nodded, Ramon went on, "Tell me something of him, Señorita Starbuck."

Jessie was silent for a moment, looking at the curiosity which Ramon's young face showed in the moonlight. Then she said, "It would be much too long a story, and our talking might disturb the others."

"But I would like to hear it," Ramon said eagerly. "And there's a place close by where we can talk without disturbing the others."

Jessie had ended her silent debate by now. She nodded and said, "Very well. We'll go there and I'll tell you about Alex."

# Chapter 3

Jessie stepped up beside Ramon as he led the way around the clump of trees where the prisoners were being held and up the slope away from the lake. They'd walked across the moonlit ground for only a few minutes when he indicated the dark blob created by a stand of young thick-leaved aspens.

"There's a little open place in the center of these trees where grass grows and where we can talk without disturbing the others," he said.

With Jessie following him now, Ramon wove his way through the trees to a grassy knoll. He gestured to the open area and stepped aside to allow Jessie to pass him and select a place to sit down, then he settled himself across from her.

"Now, tell me of your father and how he became rich," he said.

Jessie was silent for a moment. Then she said, "Alex started with almost nothing but his courage. He was an orphan, and when he was very little older than you, he went to Alaska in search of gold. He found some, not a great deal, only enough to start a small shop on the waterfront in San Francisco. I'm sure you know that's in California?"

"Certainly. I know the history of our people, Miss Starbuck. Hispanics settled California just as we have settled the land here."

"Of course." Jessie smiled. "Father's little shop sold goods from China and Japan, and he made several trips there."

"And Ki? Your father found him in China?"

"In Japan. Ki's father was an American navy officer who was among Alex's best friends and who'd married a Japanese girl from one of the old noble families. Her family disowned her, and Ki was left footloose when she and Alex's friend died in a storm at sea. Ki spent several years moving around in the Orient—that was when he learned his skill at martial arts—until Alex stumbled on him quite by accident. Then Alex brought Ki to America, where he became Alex's loyal assistant. I'm very fortunate that Ki stayed with me after my father was killed."

"He must have been a very smart man, your father," Ramon said when Jessie paused to catch her breath.

"Very smart, indeed. When he saw an opportunity, he took it, but always after finding out that he would hurt no one and would be able to improve a business without hurting anyone. He became a very rich man, and other rich men who respected his judgment began inviting him to join in their ventures, mining and banking, and—oh, many others."

"Then, business has brought you here to the territory?"

Jessie nodded. "A silver mine that was among the other businesses I inherited. It's in the southern part

27

of the territory. The superintendent of the territorial Treasury Department notified me that the mine's manager hasn't paid the usual tax on the ore extracted last year, but on one of the last reports the manager sends me each month there's an entry showing the tax has been paid."

"So you believe there are thieves either at your mine or at our treasury," Ramon said. "And you must now find out which is the case."

"Exactly. But first, Ki and I must go back to the Circle Star. We didn't expect to be delayed by bandits."

"Any more than Tío Fegeo and I expected to meet such a lovely lady on the trail while we were moving the sheep."

Ramon's voice had a tone in it that Jessie recognized at once. At different times and places she'd heard it in the voices of other men. She studied Ramon's young unlined face, his dark eyes now fixed on her features.

"That's a nice compliment, Ramon. Thank you. But don't you think we'd better get back to our bedrolls? We'll be starting early in the morning, and both of us will need all the sleep we can get."

"I won't be able to sleep for thinking of you, Jessie."

In spite of the caution signals her better judgment was sending her, Jessie kept her eyes fixed on Ramon. Before leaving for New Mexico Territory she'd been at the Circle Star for more than three months, and for the last few nights before leaving for Santa Fe her dreams had been filled with images of the lovers she'd encountered in the past. Though her mind told her that the course of wisdom dictated a return to her bedroll, the sudden tension that now began to sweep over her and grip her body was urging her to listen to her young companion's words.

"Of course you'll be able to sleep!" she said.

"And you? In this moonlight doesn't the night speak to you as it does to me?"

"But this isn't the time or the place!" she protested.

"There may never be another time or place for us!" he replied, and now there was urgency in his voice.

Ramon grasped Jessie's hand and pressed it to his lips. She felt the warm moist tip of his tongue as he ran it across her palm and a small shudder suddenly swept her body.

Ramon lifted his head and fixed his large dark eyes on hers as he asked, "Can you say now that you feel nothing for me?"

As Jessie raised her head to meet his eyes Ramon bent toward her and found her lips. In spite of her intention not to be swayed, Jessie responded when his tongue-tip parted her lips. She met his tongue with hers, and when he grasped her closer and pulled her into a firm embrace, Jessie's body quivered in an involuntary shudder.

Breathless when they at last broke the embrace, Jessie did not protest when Ramon took her hand and led her up the gentle slope. He slanted away from their sleeping companions and from the spot where the outlaws were tied and stopped at a small stand of shoulder-high *piñons*.

"We're far enough away from the others now," he said, tugging at Jessie's hand. "No one will see or hear us."

Jessie allowed Ramon to lead her into the grove. He took her in his arms again and sought her lips.

Jessie did not protest now, but met them willingly with hers. For an even longer moment than before they clung in a close embrace, tongues twisting and entwining.

Breathless at last, they broke the kiss. Ramon slipped out of his denim jacket. He spread it on the soft yielding layer of half-dry needles from the small trees and kneeled beside it, reached up and caught Jessie's hand again.

By this time she was more than willing to let Ramon take her hand and ease her to lie down on the jacket. There was no need for them to speak. When Ramon leaned over to find her lips once more, Jessie slid her hand up his thigh to find his bulging crotch and explore the swollen cylinder that her fingers found.

After a long moment of breathlessness they broke their kiss. Jessie was more than ready now. She squirmed briefly in kicking off her riding skirt and slipping out of her filmy silk pantaloons while Ramon was pushing his own jeans down his legs. She looked up at his jutting erection and quickly spread her thighs.

Ramon knelt above her. Jessie placed him and when she felt him plunge into her she brought her hips up to meet his quick jarring penetration. A throbbing sigh broke from Jessie's lips as Ramon thrust home. She locked her ankles above his back to pull him into her full-length.

Jessie held him motionless for a long shuddering breathless moment, sighing with the pleasure she'd lacked for so many weeks. After a few moments Ramon stirred and attempted to begin lunging. Jessie relaxed the grip of her tightly locked ankles and let him establish the rhythm of his thrusts. Then she caught his rhythm and joined him, bringing herself up to meet his lusty strokes each time he plunged.

After her long period of isolation on the Circle Star, Jessie did not try to delay her body's response. She built to her climax quickly. Her first small shudders of mounting ecstasy began almost at once and lasted for only a few moments before she cried out and started tossing wildly while Ramon maintained his lusty thrusts. The first shudders of ecstasy swept over her, and she gave way to them until they peaked and started to fade. While she'd been relishing her pleasure, Ramon had not lessened his steady strokes.

"Don't stop, Ramon!" she gasped into his ear.

Ramon did not reply, but continued his urgent lunges and deep, full penetrations. Jessie matched his rhythm with hers, rolling her hips as she brought them up to meet his thrusts. It seemed that only a few moments passed before she felt herself building once more. Ramon was driving faster now, and she sensed that he was also reaching the point of no return.

Jessie did not let herself go until she felt Ramon beginning to quiver with the approach of his own climax. Then as he panted and drove to the ultimate moment, she joined him while small ecstatic cries burst from her throat.

Ramon lunged for the final thrust and Jessie was already at the apex of her summit. She trembled and a stream of happy sighs poured from her lips until Ramon closed them with his own and together they shuddered and held each other close as their shudders eased and passed and they lay in silent satisfaction.

"You are indeed the woman I have been wishing for, Jessie!" Ramon whispered into her ear.

"And you're the man I've been needing for too

long a time," she replied. "Don't move for a while, Ramon. I'm enjoying just feeling you fill me."

"I would like very much never to leave you."

"It's a fine dream, but both of us know what's real. We'll enjoy what we have now, and part with a smile tomorrow. But the memory will go with us, so let's make it a fine memory while we have the chance."

Although Jessie had not returned to her bedroll until the first faint tinge of false dawn showed in the east, she woke feeling rested and refreshed when the soft brushing sounds of someone moving around reached her ears. She sat up in her blankets to look around. Elfegeo Baca was hunkered down beside the coals of last night's fire, feeding twigs into a new blaze that was just beginning to show an occasional spurt of flame.

A dim belt of darkness still lay between their camp and the dim line of the jagged horizon. A faint blatt sounded now and again from the sheep herd; the animals were beginning to scatter as they sought forage with the coming of the new day. Baca rose to his feet and saw Jessie sitting up.

"*Buenas dias*, Señorita Starbuck," he said. "I hope your sleep was enjoyable?"

"I enjoyed it very much indeed," Jessie replied.

Baca nodded, and bent low again to blow across the shallow firepit, coaxing life into the charred ends of the dead *piñon* branches that remained from last night's fire. A small huddle of twigs lay beside him, and he went back to breaking them into shorter lengths which he pushed into the flickering little blaze.

Looking around, Jessie saw Ki tossing his blankets aside. He sat up and blinked once or twice. Ramon's bedroll showed no sign of motion until Baca spoke from his place beside the shallow firepit.

"Ramon!" he called, *No permite el sol cogense en su cama! Levantase, hijo!*"

At the first sound of his uncle's voice, Ramon sat up, and before Baca had finished his admonition the young man was on his feet. He stood blinking for a moment, then nodded in a half-bow to Jessie and Ki before diving into the undergrowth.

"Breakfast will be small, I'm afraid," Baca said as he turned toward Jessie. "Ramon and I planned to reach Albuquerque, or at least Alameda, before we stopped for the night."

"There's food in our saddlebags," Jessie volunteered. "Not anything fancy, but we can share it."

Ki was already starting toward their saddle gear as Jessie spoke. He returned with a cloth-wrapped bundle, which he spread on the ground beside the small blaze that was now dancing at Baca's feet.

"This isn't much," he said. "Some sausage and tortillas, but it'll help start the day with something in our stomachs."

"Good." Baca nodded. He waited until Jessie and Ki had rolled tortillas around pieces of sausage, then helped himself. Between bites, he went on, "Too much breakfast means a slow start. We have a full day of travel, burdened as we are by the prisoners and the sheep."

"It would be worse if we were not all going in the same direction," Ramon said, moving to stand beside his uncle.

"But not at the same speed," Baca pointed out. "We have our sheep to think of. Señorita Starbuck and Ki will not want to keep to our slow pace, Ramon."

33

Jessie was also on her feet now. As she stepped closer to the fire, she said, "Ki and I didn't get as far yesterday as we'd planned, and I'm sure you didn't, either. We're anxious to get to Albuquerque, because we have to be back at my ranch for the roundup."

"I understand your need to move more rapidly than our sheep herd permits us to do," Baca replied. "A day does not matter greatly to Ramon and me. Our sheep have not yet had time to scatter badly. We will herd them together very quickly and be moving again."

"And by the time Ki and I get back to the trail, we should be able to see well enough to follow it," Jessie went on.

"You will have no trouble," Baca said. "There are only two small creeks to cross before you reach Albuquerque."

"Even if we could stay with you, I'm afraid Ki and I wouldn't be much help to you," Jessie told him. "We understand cattle and their ways, but sheep are strange animals to both of us. Instead of helping, we'd probably just be in your way."

"These are things we all understand," Baca said, nodding. "We have met and become friends, we part as friends and perhaps will meet again. Now, I know that you and Ki wish to make haste, Señorita Starbuck. Go with God and our best wishes that you reach your rancho safely."

"Except for the sheep, and the duty I have to help Tío Fegeo with his prisoners, I would like nothing better than to go with you and show you the way," Ramon put in.

"Much as I appreciate the thought, I'm afraid it's not very practical," Jessie told him. "But perhaps we'll meet again, Ramon. And we're grateful for the help you and your uncle gave us. Now, let's finish our breakfast and be on our way. There's a full day ahead for all of us."

"I think I'm almost too tired to believe that we're home at last, Ki," Jessie confessed as they topped the little rise and saw the cluster of the Circle Star's buildings on the broad level floor of the shallow valley ahead. "I'm always glad to get back home, but this time I'm especially glad. I'm sure you must feel like I do, that we've been dragged by our heels through a brier patch these last few days."

"Yes. It wasn't a particularly happy trip in some respects," Ki agreed. "Now, in addition to the roundup, we've got the Silver City problem to take care of."

"I think we'd be wise to let that rest until after the roundup, Ki. What I need right now is a bath and a restful night's sleep in my own bed."

"Well, they're both within sight," Ki said. "And I'll be as glad as you are to be at home again."

"We'll get through the roundup," Jessie went on, a thoughtful frown on her face. "Get the market herd cut out and ready. Then we'll worry about the mine and Silver City."

Ki nodded. "The men will need a few days to chouse the steers we're keeping back to the grazing ranges."

"They'll have plenty of time to do that before we ship," Jessie went on. "You and I can rest for the next few days, until the cattle cars we've ordered get to the siding. Then we'll have to drive the market steers to the railroad and load the cars, but that's just a routine job, one we're used to."

"And you intend to go to Silver City after the market herd's been shipped?"

"Of course. I haven't any idea why Bob Jernigan should be stealing from the mine, because for the past few years he's been paid quite generously. And he's been with me long enough to know that if he needs money all he has to do is ask for a loan or for an advance in his salary."

"There's no way of knowing why people like him go wrong, Jessie. And it's always a shock to find out that someone you've trusted for a long time has been stealing from you."

"That's something I'm not going to worry about until the roundup's finished and the market herd's on its way."

"Everything after that is just routine, things Ed Wright can handle."

"Of course," Jessie said with a nod.

She fell silent as they reined into the broad stretch of ground between the big house and the ranch's working buildings: bunkhouse, cookhouse, barns, stables, and beyond them the horse corrals. Ed Wright, the Circle Star foreman, had obviously seen them approaching, for he was standing in front of the cookshack waiting.

"It's good to see you and Ki back, Miss Jessie," he said. "I spotted you and Ki a little while back and figured I might as well be here to set your mind at rest, if you've been wondering how things are. We've begun to shape up the market herd, and the station agent says the cars will be waiting at the siding when you're ready to ship."

"That's good news, Ed," Jessie replied as she swung out of her saddle.

"Sun's hoof's better, too," Wright went on. "But

it's going to be another few days before you can ride him free and easy."

"Then he'll be as glad to get out of his stall as I will to swing into his saddle," Jessie said.

"I won't bother you with anything more right now," the foreman went on. "You and Ki will want to be getting freshened up, and Gimpy's got a hot supper waiting for you whenever you're ready to sit down."

"Tell him to bring it right on over, then," Jessie said. "Ki's as tired and hungry as I am, and we'll be ready to get a meal of his good cooking."

Jessie and Ki had settled down in the big room at the Circle Star that had been Alex Starbuck's study. It was the room Jessie preferred above all others at the Circle Star, for it still bore the characteristics imparted to it by her father.

It was a big room, with a fieldstone fireplace dominating one wall, a life-size oil portrait of Jessie's long-dead mother on another, and a similar portrait of her father facing it from the opposite wall. The furniture bore Alex Starbuck's stamp as well. The battered rolltop desk which had been in the office of his first small curio shop on the San Francisco waterfront stood in a corner of the room beyond Alex's portrait.

Jessie liked to nestle into one of the big leather-upholstered chairs, or stretch out on the divan that occupied the space in front of the fireplace. It was her fancy that even so many years after her father's tragic and untimely death that when she was on the divan or in one of the chairs, she could still smell the fragrance of Alex's favorite pipe tobacco. She was curled up in one of the chairs now, while Ki occupied a corner of the divan.

"I'm more than ready for bed," Ki said. "So I'll say good night and—" He broke off as a knock sounded at the outer door. "I'll see who that is. Probably one of the hands who's got some kind of problem."

While Ki was out of the room, Jessie stretched luxuriously on the divan. She heard the thunking of bootheels, a signal that Ki was bringing the visitor back with him. The newcomer entered the room first, a big hulking man carrying a wide-brimmed Stetson and wearing denim jeans with their legs tucked into scuffed-up boots.

"This is Harry Walters, Jessie," Ki told Jessie. "A Texas Ranger. He has some news I know you'll want to hear."

Jessie nodded as she said, "Of course, if it concerns the Circle Star. What is your news, Mr. Walters?"

"It's about your ranch all right, Miss Starbuck," Walters said. "I've got some real dependable information that there's a gang of rustlers on the way here to steal your market herd."

# Chapter 4

For a moment all that Jessie could do was stare, then she said, "I don't know or care where you got your information, but I'm sure you wouldn't have come here unless you're positive that it's right. But you can certainly count on us to help you. I'm not going to stand by quietly while a bunch of outlaws steal my steers!"

"I was sorta figuring that's what you'd say, Miss Starbuck," Walters said.

"Come in and sit down, Mr. Walters," Jessie went on. "I want to find out more about this bunch of cattle rustlers."

While Walters moved to the chair she'd indicated, Jessie took stock of their unexpected visitor. The broad-brimmed hat he carried in one hand was a range worker's Stetson, the sort of battered sweat-stained headgear that a cowhand would be wearing. His boots were well-worn, but not as scuffed-up as those of a cattle wrangler forced to dig his boot heels into the hard prairie soil to brace himself against a taut lariat with an angry steer at the other end. Walters's head was a bit too big for his body and his hands bore none of the rope-burn scars or crooked fingers which were the marks of a working cowboy, though a wide crooked scar ran across his right cheek.

"I don't like to bust in on a ranch when I know it's either roundup time or close to it," Walters said as he settled into the chair Jessie had indicated. "But what I had to tell you couldn't wait."

"Of course not. It's important and I certainly want to hear the details," Jessie told him. "But I'm also inclined to be careful."

A puzzled frown formed on Walters's face as he said, "Maybe I don't take your meaning, ma'am."

"I'd just like to see your badge," Jessie replied. "I've found that the first thing most lawmen do is to prove they're who they say they are."

"Well, you're sure right about that, Miss Starbuck. I oughta showed you my badge right off, but I wanted to explain first why I'm here."

Walters was pulling out a much-worn leather wallet as he spoke. He flipped it open and held it up for Jessie to look at. She saw the familiar badge and even at a distance could read his name on the silver circle that enclosed the Texas star.

"Thank you," Jessie said. "It's not that I doubted you, but I've learned to be careful."

"And I sure don't blame you," Walters agreed.

"Now, just what is it that's brought you here, Mr. Walters?" Jessie went on.

"There's two parts to the case I'm here about. One is to keep you from having a lot of your cattle rustled, and the other one is to catch the rustling gang in the act and put 'em out of business for good."

40

"I'm certainly on your side in both of your aims," Jessie assured him. "Cattle thieves haven't bothered the Circle Star lately, but they do pop up. What is it you want me to do?"

"I take it you've shipped your herd out by now? And there's not much left on your range but breeder and scrub cattle?"

Jessie frowned. "We don't run scrubs on the Circle Star."

"No offense meant, ma'am," Walters said quickly. "You see, I don't know too much about your spread here, except that it's a right good-sized one."

"And we've just finished our roundup," Jessie went on. "It'll take several weeks of good hard work before we'll be ready to cut out the steers for the market herd."

"I'm sure glad I got here when I did," Walters said. "You'll still have time, then."

"Time for what?" she asked. She shook her head a bit impatiently and added quickly, "I'm afraid I'll have to apologize if I seem a bit impatient, Mr. Walters. Ki and I have just gotten back from New Mexico Territory. We ran into a bit of trouble there, and we've had a very hurried trip home."

"Now, that's something I can understand," Walters said, nodding. "I get a little bit tetchy myself when things don't go right. You don't need to make any apologies."

"Your visit is such a surprise that I'm afraid I neglected to ask you whether you've had your supper yet," she went on. "Ki and I came in on the last train, and since I didn't see you in the dining car, I'm sure you must be hungry. And if there's a restaurant anywhere close by, I'm not aware of it."

Walters acknowledged Jessie's mild joke by smiling before settling down into the chair she'd indicated and placing his hat beside it.

"Thanks for the offer, Miss Starbuck," he replied. "But I'm not hungry. I finished off my saddle rations while I was riding across your range on the way here."

"I'm a bit surprised that Ki and I didn't see you on the train," Jessie went on.

"Oh, I wasn't on the train. I rode cross-country."

"You must've had quite a ride, then," Ki put in.

"Sure, but I wanted to see how the land lays hereabouts, so I just followed my map. I've heard your place here's a good stretch from the railroad line, and figured I'd save time riding cross-country. But getting here took longer than I figured."

"It's a long ride from anywhere to get here," Jessie agreed. "But we're used to the distance. My father built this house before the railroad line was surveyed, and though they promised to bring the line fairly close, something went wrong with their survey."

Ki had been following the conversation between Jessie and the newcomer. Now he broke in to volunteer, "Even if you aren't hungry, I'm sure you'd like some coffee. Or tea—we have both."

"Coffee would taste real good right now," Walters said.

Ki nodded and turned to Jessie to ask, "Which do you want, Jessie?"

"Coffee will be fine," she replied. Turning back to Walters as Ki started for the kitchen, she went on, "I'm anxious to hear this important news you've brought me, but let's wait until Ki comes back before you start. Then neither of us will have to waste time repeating it."

"I hope you won't take offense at something that's

digging away at my curiosity, Miss Starbuck, but ain't that sorta unusual?" Walters frowned. "A servant listening to a private talk like I was figuring to have with you?"

"Ki isn't a servant, Mr. Walters," Jessie answered. "In fact, he doesn't really fit neatly into any classification. He was my father's confidential assistant, and I suppose that's as close as you can come to describing the place he fills for me here on the Circle Star as well as in my other enterprises."

"Well, now, if I've said the wrong thing, I'm real sorry," Walters told her hastily. "No offense meant, Miss Starbuck."

"And none taken," Jessie assured him.

At that moment Ki returned, carrying a tray which held steaming cups. He served Jessie and Walters in turn, then carried his own cup to a chair at one side of the divan and settled down near Jessie.

"Now, you've had time to catch your breath after your long ride, Mr. Walters," Jessie said. "Suppose you tell us what's brought you here."

"I guess on a ranch as big as this one, you'd have about the biggest market herd in Texas, Miss Starbuck," Walters began.

"Perhaps not the biggest," Jessie said with a frown. "The LX up in the Panhandle runs about as many head of cattle as the Circle Star. So does Colonel Goodnight, if you count the range he has over in New Mexico Territory. And there's the Kleberg outfit, down on the Gulf Coast, and—"

"Excuse me, Miss Starbuck," Walters said apologetically. "None of those ranchers are concerned with what I've come to talk to you about."

"Of course," Jessie replied. "I didn't mean to break in on what you were saying. Please, go ahead."

Walters nodded and went on, "Now, I'd imagine you've got a pretty good idea about how we do our job in the Rangers. We try to keep a jump ahead of the killers and rustlers and other kinds of crooks. We get a lot of news from all over everywhere, from lawmen and even from crooks that've had some sort of falling out with another bad one. That's how we found out about some plans that a new gang of rustlers has worked out."

Jessie frowned as she said, "I don't think I quite understand what you're getting at, Mr. Walters."

"Well, you know how it is with the Rangers right now, I guess?"

"Perhaps I don't know as much as I should," Jessie said. "But surely the Ranger force hasn't changed a great deal."

Walters frowned. "That depends on how much you'd call a great deal, I guess. What I'm talking about is the old days when Rangers rode in companies, like cavalry in the army, Miss Starbuck. You'd know that there's not all that many of us on the roster these days, I suppose."

"Yes, of course," Jessie said, nodding. "But I've always thought of the Rangers as being a fairly sizable force, Texas being such a big state."

"Most folks have got the same idea," Walters agreed. "But what I'm trying to say is that not too long back there was a Ranger stationed in every county seat. In counties that've got big towns like San Antonio and Fort Worth and Dallas, there'd be maybe three or four Rangers. It's not that way anymore. The politicians in Austin say that tax money's not coming in the way it used to, so they started squeezing us."

For the first time since he'd returned to the room,

Ki spoke. He said, "So what you're saying is that the Ranger force today isn't as large as it was a few years ago."

Walters nodded. "That's just what I'm getting at. The way it is right now, there's maybe just one Ranger for every two or three counties."

"Doesn't that spread your force terribly thin?" Jessie asked with a frown.

"Sure it does," Walters replied. "That's why I've come to talk to you, Miss Starbuck. What I'm trying to get around to is telling you that we're having to call on good citizens like you when we need to get them to lend us a hand."

"I'll be glad to, of course," Jessie said unhesitatingly. "But I'm curious to know what kind of help you'll need."

"What I aim to do is set a trap for the rustlers," he told her. "I figure we can—"

"Excuse me for interrupting you," Jessie said, the small frown that had formed on her face becoming more pronounced. "But are you absolutely sure that this gang has picked the Circle Star as their target?"

"I sure am," Walters answered. "We haven't got all the ins and outs of their scheme yet, but that's why I'm here."

"To warn us, I suppose?"

"That's the main reason, Miss Starbuck," Walters agreed. "But what I'm getting at goes a ways past just tipping you off to be on the lookout for trouble."

"Perhaps you'd better start at the beginning," Jessie suggested. "Naturally, I'm curious to find out what you've uncovered about this scheme to rustle my cattle, but I'm even more interested in learning what you expect me to do to help you."

"Well, now," Walters said, frowning, "there's not

much use in me going back too far except to say that this gang I've been talking about is big and mean."

"Most outlaw gangs are," Ki said when their visitor stopped for a moment. "But from what you're hinting at, Mr. Walters, this new bunch of outlaws must be especially vicious."

"They are," Walters agreed. "Killers and cutthroats. But they're as smart as they are mean and greedy. We want to break them up before they get any stronger."

"How many men are there in the gang?" Jessie asked. "Ten? Twenty?"

"That's something we can't be sure of. They're copying the way Jesse James and his brother worked for such a long time. They get together and pull a big job, then they scatter. Some go one way, some another."

"But surely you've got witnesses to the jobs they've already pulled?" Jessie said.

"Not too many. So far they've only raided two little towns and a couple of ranches, and everybody who's lasted through one of their raids tells a different story about how many men are in the outfit."

"Isn't that a little bit strange?" Jessie asked.

"Not awfully, Miss Starbuck," Walters replied, shaking his head. "Mostly these outlaws work in the dark. They'll swoop down just about sunset and be gone before daylight, so there's always five or six different stories about the size of the bunch."

"Suppose you get down to cases, Mr. Walters," Jessie suggested. "Then tell us what the gang intends to do to the Circle Star. When I know that, we can begin to make some plans."

"I was hoping you'd say something like that," Walters told her. "Because what this outfit figures to do is real important to you. They're planning to steal your whole market herd."

Jessie did not reply for a moment. A thoughtful frown had formed on her face. At last she said, "You're talking about a very large herd of steers, Mr. Walters."

"Oh, I figured that out for myself even before I started here," he said. "I didn't have much to go by, but your Circle Star market herd must be one of the biggest in Texas."

"It's large," Jessie agreed. "And represents a great deal of money. Losing it wouldn't cripple me, or anything like that, but it's something I don't propose to let happen."

"I'm curious to know how you managed to find out so much about this bunch of outlaws and their plans," Ki put in. "Usually when a bunch of crooks are working up to a job this size, they'll be very careful to keep anybody from finding out what they're going to do."

"Of course," Walters said, nodding. "And I'm going to beg off from telling you the way I got the information. It's not that I've got any doubts about you or Miss Starbuck, but if anything about it could spill out, the gang might find out about it."

"Yes, I can understand that," Jessie agreed. "And you can depend on Ki and me to keep very quiet about whatever you choose to tell us."

"I was figuring that's what you'd most likely say. The truth of it is that I been counting on your help pretty strong."

"You'll have it, of course," Jessie replied promptly. "Just tell me what you need."

"I'm glad to see you ain't like some folks, Miss Starbuck," Walters said. "They get mad when a man in my situation has to ask 'em questions about their private affairs."

"That's never bothered me," Jessie told him. "It's one of the many lessons I learned from my father. He always said that people who're too close-mouthed about their private lives are trying to hide something they're ashamed of."

"I reckon he's right about that," Walters agreed.

"I don't suppose you ever ran across my father," Jessie said. "Alexander Starbuck?"

"Well, I've sure heard the name, but I never have had the pleasure of meeting him." Walters frowned. "Not that I wouldn't like to, if you're figuring on asking him to come in and give us some advice."

"My father is dead, Mr. Walters. He was murdered."

"Well, I'm right sorry to hear that. I hope the fellow that did it got what was coming to him."

"It wasn't a fellow. A gang of hired killers did it. And in one way or another, his death has been avenged."

"Then the law caught up with 'em," Walters said.

"Let's say justice was given to them," Ki amended. He fell silent, for he was recalling the day when Alex Starbuck had asked him to make a trip to the whistle-stop depot to send an important telegram, and Jessie's father had been assassinated.

Jessie had also remained silent after her exchange with Walters. The very mention of Alex Starbuck had brought back memories that were painful treasures. This time the memory was not a pleasant one, for it invoked the picture of her father having been killed on the Circle Star's western range by a band of murderers hired by the European cartel which had been trying to pirate America's rich resources to revive their nations' fading strengths.

At the time of Alex's murder, Jessie had been away from the Circle Star, at the fashionable Eastern finishing school in which Alex had enrolled her. She'd had no hint of the reason for Alex's murder until Ki had brought the bad news to her. It was then, in the space of a few hours, that Jessie had reached maturity and had made her own resolution to avenge her father's murder by taking up the battle he'd begun with the cartel.

Ki at that time had been serving as Alex's confidential assistant as well as defending him from the attacks of the cartel. He'd stayed at Jessie's side during the long period of mourning which followed, a span that had covered almost two full years. During those years Jessie had for the first time learned the full scope of the far-flung industrial and financial empire that Alex had built before the cartel had invited him to join its ranks.

To Jessie's surprise she'd discovered that her inheritance included vast stands of timber in the Pacific Northwest, and substantial tracts of agricultural lands in the rich valleys of California and the prairies of the central states. In addition to these there were such other tangible assets as gold and silver mines both in the West and in Alaska, as well as stockholdings in banks and brokerage houses in the three major financial centers of the country.

Alex had chosen to live in the West, where he'd started his meteoric career, and the Circle Star had been intended by him to be a place where he could go to find rest and relief from the hurly-burly of the industrial and financial world.

Although Jessie's mental journey through the past

had taken up only a few moments, she suddenly became aware that both Walters and Ki had fallen silent as well. She broke the silence by turning to Walters and asking, "Now, is there anything more that we need to discuss right at the moment, Mr. Walters? Or can we wait until tomorrow to make the rest of our plans?"

"Why, the kind of information you've been giving me is what I've needed more than anything else," Walters said. He stifled a yawn as he went on, "You've filled in a lot of gaps already. I imagine there'll be a few more before we can figure out the best way to round up these crooks and capture 'em."

"It's lucky that Ki and I have time to spend with you right now," Jessie said. She turned to Ki and went on, "It seems that we timed getting back from our trip just right."

"It couldn't have been better," Ki agreed. "We'll be ready, and if we're lucky we can give those rustlers the kind of welcome they're not expecting."

"Yes, it's all to the good," Walters agreed. He stood up and went on, "I suppose there's an empty bed in your bunkhouse where I can sleep while I'm here? Two or three nights ought to see that gang ride up."

"There's always room on the Circle Star for unexpected guests," Jessie assured him. "But there's plenty of room here in the main house."

"Well, now, I'm obliged for your invitation, Miss Starbuck," Walters replied. "But your bunkhouse is the place for me to be while I'm here. I'd like to size up your hands, have them get used to me at the same time."

"Of course," Jessie said, nodding. "I can see your reasons. Ki will take you out and see that you're comfortable. We can finish our talk later. Instead of eating with the hands, join Ki and me for breakfast. After we've eaten, you and I will ride out and I'll show you the Circle Star range."

# Chapter 5

"I was hoping that's what you'd say, Miss Starbuck," Walters told Jessie. "But if you don't mind spending a few more minutes, there's two or three more little things that we oughta talk about right now."

"Of course," Jessie agreed. "Go ahead."

"I've already mentioned that I don't know much about this part of Texas—it's strange country to me," Walters said. "Mostly I've been farther east. And I don't have any idea which way the gang will be coming from, or how many men there'll be. I do have one bit of information that might be helpful, though."

"I hope it's something you can share with us," Jessie said when Walters did not continue immediately.

"I'd be foolish not to share it," he replied.

"And Jessie or I would be equally foolish if we let anything leak out about your sources of information or about whatever plan you have in mind," Ki pointed out.

"I understand that," Walters agreed. "In fact, that's one of the things I've been counting on."

"That's settled," Jessie said. "Now that we've agreed, where do we start?"

"It's hard to know just where to begin," Walters told her. He fell silent for a moment, frowning thoughtfully. At last he said, "There are a few more things that're on my question list, Miss Starbuck. You've got a real big spread here. I'm guessing you've got two or three line camps, maybe more."

"Of course. We have five of them, as a matter of fact. They're not elaborate, if you're thinking about rustlers using them to hide out in."

"Well, it wouldn't be the first time that's happened."

"So I've heard," Jessie said. "But here on the Circle Star we've got so much range to cover that our line shacks are almost always occupied. The men take turns, but generally there will be a hand close by."

"Riding in, I got to figuring how a gang of rustlers might pick a place to make their moves, but then it occurred to me that I don't know beans from breakfast about where your steers are going to be."

"That's something I haven't planned yet. Is it very important for you to know it now?"

"There's no one thing more important than the others; it's what they all add up to. Mostly it's bits and scraps of things I don't know about. One of them is how the land lays on the range where you're holding your market herd."

"We haven't formed the full herd yet. Usually we hold it on the east range, because the prairie's nice and level between it and the railroad."

"Yes, I noticed that riding in here," Walters said,

then went on, "Now, I'm wondering if you've hired on any new hands lately, to take care of the extra work that a roundup always makes on a ranch."

Jessie shook her head. "We keep pretty much the same number of hands regardless of the season. And all the men on the payroll now have been working on the Circle Star for—well, I guess it's been at least five months, closer to six, since I've hired anybody new."

"Then we won't have to worry about the rustlers having somebody here to give them any kind of advance information. Unless they've got somebody planted on your ranch as a spy, they won't have any hints about me coming here to warn you of their plans. That means they won't know they're getting into a trap."

"As long as Ki and I are the only ones who know why you're here, the hands will think you're just another drifter," Jessie assured him.

"Then, my third question is when you're due to ship your cattle," Walters said.

"I'm afraid that's the question I can't answer," Jessie replied. "Usually it'll take two days to drive our market steers from the holding range to the railroad siding. We were supposed to get word from the SP's stationmaster at least a week before the cars would be here. So far, we haven't heard from him."

"You're expecting to get word pretty soon, though?"

"Almost any day, I'd say," Jessie said. "But we don't have to start the herd moving at once. We can delay that for a day or so, if that would fit into your plans better."

"I haven't made any real plans yet," Walters said with a frown. "So we'll wait to work out the details until I've looked over your range. But I feel better about this case now than I did when I first found out how big your spread is."

"And that's all you wanted to know?" Jessie asked.

"It is for right now. Later on I'll be asking about the rest of what I need to know."

"Then would you mind telling me something?"

"Of course not."

"How does it happen that you know so much about this gang of outlaws?"

"I took one of them prisoner," Walters replied. "He swapped information in return for getting off easier than he would have otherwise."

"I see," Jessie said. "Now, do you mind if I make a suggestion?"

"Of course not. It's your ranch and your cattle we're talking about."

"If we have as much time as you think we will, wouldn't it be better to ride around a bit and see for yourself what the range is like?" Jessie asked. "There might be some places on the Circle Star, especially the area around the holding range, that you'd want to look at pretty closely."

"First-hand knowledge is always better than second-hand," Walters agreed. "Yes, I'd like to see your holding range in daylight, Miss Starbuck. I'll have to know the lay of the land to figure out which way the rustlers are most likely to come from and which way they might be expected to drive the herd they're planing to steal. And if it's not too much of a ride, I'd like to see some of the country to the southeast of here."

When Jessie heard Walters's last few words, a frown began forming on her face. It deepened as she said, "I'm guessing now. But is that the direction you think the rustlers plan to move my cattle after they've stolen them?"

"Toward Mexico?" Ki added before Walters had a chance to respond to Jessie's question.

"There's no way that I can be sure the gang will head for the Rio Grande," Walters replied. "But it'd make sense. Our jurisdiction ends at the river, even if some of the boys slip across it now and again. But like I said a minute ago, right now us Rangers aren't getting along too well with the Rurales on the other side of the river."

After a moment of silence, Jessie went on, "Tell us what help you need, then. Either from me or Ki or both of us or from our hands."

"Information like you've just been giving me is what I've needed more than anything else. You've filled in the gaps, but I'm sure there'll be others to open up later. All I can see right now is just waiting."

"It's lucky that the roundup and cutting-out jobs are finished," Jessie said. "Right now Ki and I have plenty of time to spend with you."

"And that's all to the good," Walters said. He stifled a yawn as he went on, "Seems like it's about time for me to turn in. If you'll point out the way to your bunkhouse—"

"You won't change your mind about sleeping out there?" Jessie asked, honoring the old Texas tradition of giving an unexpected guest a second chance to agree or to refuse. "As I said, there's plenty of room right here in the main house."

"Thanks, ma'am, but I'll be helping my job by getting a look at your hands. Even if you don't have any drifters on your payroll, those outlaws might've bought off one of your regular hands, and if they have I'll be trying to sniff it out."

"I don't think that's a very likely possibility," Jessie said with a frown. "There are only a couple of them who've been here for just a short time, five or six months. The old hands would never get involved with anything crooked, I'm sure of that."

"Well, a man in my position can't afford to take unnecessary chances. If I'm in with your men, I'll be better able to judge them, and that could be right important."

"Yes, I realize that," Jessie told him. "And it reminds me that Ki and I will have to be careful and treat you like you're just a run-of-the mill drifter."

"That's the ticket, all right," Walters agreed. "But I bet you're getting tired of all this talking we've been doing. I'd better be getting out to your bunkhouse, or your hands will be wondering why I'm spending such a long time in here talking to you and Ki."

Before she could ask him, Ki spoke up. "I'll take Mr. Walters out to the bunkhouse, Jessie. And while we're outside, we'll put his horse in the corral, too."

As Ki rose, Walters also got to his feet. He said, "I'm sure I don't need to caution you and Ki, but it'll be better if you just don't pay any sort of attention to me while I'm around here, Miss Starbuck. As far as you're concerned, I'm just a drifter passing through who stopped to ask for a job."

"Don't worry," she assured him. "We'll be very careful. I'll only tell our foreman who you are. It's not unusual for drifters to stay around a day or so, resting and getting a few square meals."

Walters frowned. "It'd be better if I have an excuse

for staying, though. Suppose I say that my horse acted like it was going lame?"

"It's as good a reason as any," Jessie agreed. "There are plenty of spare horses in the holding corral. If you need one, ask Ed Wright—my foreman."

"I'm usually in and out of the bunkhouse several times a day," Ki went on. "If you have any news for Jessie, just pass it on to me."

"That's the best arrangement," Jessie agreed. "And until all the danger's past, both Ki and I will be right here on the Circle Star, ready to give you any help you might need."

"I'll be going, then," Walters said. "And as soon as I've had a day or so to get familiar with your ranch's layout, we'll figure out a way for you to show me how the land lays beyond your main house here."

After Walters had left for the bunkhouse, Jessie turned to Ki and said, "It looks like we'll have to put off our trip to Silver City."

"I've been thinking that myself," Ki said. "But even if this rustling threat hadn't come up, we couldn't have started until the market herd's on its way to the Fort Worth stockyards."

"Oh, I'm not complaining," Jessie said quickly. "I can use the extra time going over the mine's books and finding out how and when Bob Jernigan's been doing his stealing."

"And it'll give us a chance to rest a bit," Ki said. "There's not much we can do about planning a surprise reception for that rustler gang the Ranger's after until he tells us more about what we can expect."

"He seems to know a great deal about them already."

"Which ought to be to our advantage," Ki said.

"So now we'll just have to play a waiting game and see if we can have a real surprise for them when they get here."

"I think the best way for you to get an idea of the Circle Star's layout fixed in your mind is for us to start riding south," Jessie said to Walters the next morning as they started their mounts at a walk away from the horse corral. "I've been thinking about directions we might take since Ki handed me your note while I was down here earlier looking at Sun."

"That'd be the big palomino I was admiring in the little corral he's got all to hisself?" Walters asked. "I sorta figured he might be your favorite horse."

"He is," Jessie said. "Somehow he managed to wedge a stone in the frog of one hoof, and it's lamed him for a few days."

"So it's not real bad," Walters said. "It'd be a shame for anything to happen to a fine animal like that."

"He'll be all right in a day or two. But to get back to the reason for this ride, I'd imagine you're looking for the ways—or maybe I'd better say the directions—these outlaws might take in coming to the ranch?"

"Coming and going both," Walters said. "And one's about as important as the other. From what little I've managed to find out about this bunch, they're pretty smart. They'd likely come at the ranch one way and figure to get away in some other direction. It'll help me to know the lay of the land."

They'd made a slow ambling ride from the main house in the generally southeasterly direction Jessie had chosen after Ki passed on the scribbled note which Walters had slipped him as they met by chance at the big corral soon after breakfast.

It was late enough in the morning now for the sun to be out of their eyes, and both Jessie and Walters were wearing wide-brimmed hats that shielded their faces from its rays. They'd reached the rounded curving crest of a little upslope and Jessie reined in. She looked back toward the ranch buildings.

Only the roofs of the bunkhouse and cookshack were visible, but the topmost sections of the big barn and the two-story main house could still be seen in silhouette above the horizon line behind them. When Walters pulled up his mount beside her, Jessie turned in her saddle and waved her hand at the vista ahead.

"This is one of the few high spots on my range," she said. "It's not too high, but we don't have time to ride to the actual boundary lines, and you can get a pretty good idea of what it's like to the south and east."

"Whatever you say, Miss Starbuck," Walters agreed. "I don't suppose there's anybody around who'd be a better guide."

"Ki and I talked about this ride today when I'd read the note you slipped him after breakfast," Jessie replied. "He knows the ranch as thoroughly as I do. He's ridden it many times with my father when Alex was dividing it up into separate ranges."

"Well, I had a reason for wanting to take this ride so soon," Walters went on. "Like I mentioned when we was first talking, I got a hunch that the rustler gang is figuring to drive your herd to Mexico. It'd be a lot easier for them to stay clear of the law, south of the Rio Grande."

"They won't get as much for the cattle, though."

"Well, Miss Starbuck, I'd imagine they figure just

like all the rustlers I've ever run across. They got the steers without putting out a penny on 'em, so whatever they sell 'em for is cash money, free and clear."

"I've heard that cattle-thief saying before," Jessie said. "But I don't agree with it, of course."

Walters waved his hand toward the next rise and said, "I'd guess that ridge up ahead is about a good half-hour's ride, but you'd know that better than I do."

"If we were to ride to the top of it, you'd see that the land levels out for quite a distance," she explained. "There are a few low spots in it. Most of them are old buffalo wallows, and they're generally nothing more than small dips."

"And the rest of your range is generally level, like the stretch ahead?"

"All of it," Jessie replied. "But it doesn't hold the little bit of water it gets from the occasional rainshower that falls. A big rain will just be swallowed. There aren't any ranches in it, or any settlements or towns, if that's what you're wondering about."

"Well, you see, Miss Starbuck, all I know about what's ahead is the ideas I got from studying my map."

"It's just deserted country," Jessie told him. "When my father first put the Circle Star together, he looked at the land to the southeast and decided it wasn't worth buying. I've only been over for a few miles, and don't really know what it's like beyond there. But from the little I saw, I'm sure a herd of cattle could be driven in that direction."

"Clear to the Rio Grande?"

"Oh, certainly. It's a level wide pass between the Davis Mountains and the Santiago Mountains.

They're low ranges, of course, nothing like the big peaks in the Rockies or the Sierra Nevadas."

"And you're sure there's no kind of settlement in it?"

"None that I know of. As I think I told you, there are three or four ranches south of the Circle Star that sell their market herds in Mexico, but I don't sell my steers there. I've found I can ship them on the railroad and get a better price from the stockyards in Fort Worth."

"How long do you figure it'd take to drive your cattle to where they can cross the Rio Grande?" Walters asked.

Jessie was silent for a moment, then she asked thoughtfully, "Do you mean at some place where the rustlers could cross without anybody seeing them?"

Walters nodded and added, "In daylight, of course."

"Two or three weeks, with luck. Did you have any special place in mind?"

"Almost anyplace between the big bend in the Rio Grande and the mouth of the Pecos."

"That covers a lot of ground."

Jessie nodded. "It's a stretch of almost a hundred miles where there aren't any towns and no ranches to speak of. The rustlers could very easily ride around places where they might run into people who'd ask questions."

Walters repeated his earlier question, "And you figure it'd take two or three weeks to get to the river?"

"If I had a good outfit, like the one my hands on the Circle Star have turned into, I'd almost be willing to guarantee that I could get a good-sized herd to the nearest Rio Grande crossing in two weeks, give or take a day or so. I might even make it in less time, if I wanted to push them."

Walters was silent for a moment, then he said, "I don't know how familiar you are with rustlers, Miss Starbuck—"

Jessie broke in, "I think I've already mentioned that we've had a few problems with them on the Circle Star, and we've always managed to come out on top."

"Then I've probably run into more rustling outfits than you have," he went on. "And I've learned that unless they're as green as this range we're riding over, they're a lot better at moving a herd fast than any bunch of thirty-dollar a month ranch hands. When they're driving a herd of stolen cattle, they've got to move those steers in a hurry unless they want to wind up with their necks in a noose and their feet kicking in the air."

"Yes, I can understand that," Jessie said, nodding. "But now that you've seen the way the land lies between here and the Rio Grande, do you want to push ahead any farther? Or shall we turn around and go back to the Circle Star?"

"Oh, I don't think we want to do that," Walters replied. "I'm curious about a couple of the things I see in that long clear space ahead of us."

Jessie frowned. "I guess I don't remember the area you're talking about."

She turned in her saddle to look ahead of them. The sun was climbing. Walters was reining his mount closer to her when she turned. Then Jessie felt the pressure of cold steel on the back of her neck. Her hand started dropping to the butt of her holstered Colt, but before she could reach the pistol, Walters's cold menacing voice stopped her movement.

"Now, I wouldn't do that, Miss Starbuck," he said. "Even if you're worth more to me alive than you'd be dead, I'd still figure a way to collect a pretty sizable chunk of cash if I was to promise I'd bring you back safe and sound."

During the long dangerous years when she and Ki had been battling the merciless killers responsible for the death of her father, Jessie had learned many things. Among them was the total self-control required to survive such threats as the one she now faced.

"From what you've just said, I gather that you're not who you claimed to be," she told her captor. Her voice was as cool and unruffled as though they were having an informal chat across a dinner table.

"You sure hit it right that time," Walters replied. "And we won't be going back to your fancy ranch, if you haven't figured that out yet."

"This isn't the first time I've been held at gunpoint, and I don't like the idea of getting killed. Tell me what you want me to do, and I'll follow your instructions."

"Now, that's what I call being smart," Walters said. "And I don't aim to turn you into dead meat unless I've got to. Now, just behave nice and you won't get hurt."

# Chapter 6

"I ain't seen Miss Jessie around since sometime this morning, Ki," Ed Wright said as he and Ki reached the mess hall door at the same time when they were starting outside after supper.

"I haven't, either," Ki replied. "And she may not be back until after dark. I've just told cookie to save some supper for her and that Texas Ranger."

"Out on the range with him, is she? And you didn't go along?"

"Not this time. They were just going out to scout around. Walters wanted to get the lay of the land."

"That ranger's a close-mouthed son of a gun, I'll give him that much," Wright went on as he and Ki stopped on the earth-beaten stretch between the mess hall and the main house. "When he come in last night, I tried to talk with him, make him feel like he was welcome. He was polite and all that, but he sure don't waste a lot of words."

"I noticed that when he was talking to Jessie and me," Ki said, nodding.

Wright was silent for a moment. An expression more puzzled than worried was forming on his face. At last he went on, "It's not that I'm trying to poke my nose into Miss Jessie's business, Ki, you know that ain't my style. But I feel like I sorta got to ask you, did that ranger come here looking for somebody special? I can't help wondering if he's after one of them new wranglers we hired on for the gathers."

"He has a good reason for being here, Ed," Ki replied. "You don't have to worry about it having anything to do with our men. He's after a gang that's been busy over in the central part of the state. He says the outlaws are supposed to be heading this way."

"Rustlers?" Wright frowned, "They've sorta shied away from the Circle Star for quite a while. But I guess they're like the seven-year itch, you don't get 'em for a long time, then they pop up outa no place and it's hell to get rid of 'em."

"From the little bit Walters has told Jessie and me, they're rustlers, bank robbers, and I'm sure there are some killers in the bunch. He hasn't really said a great deal about them, except that he's here to get rid of them. But I'll ask you not to spread the word about that among the men. As soon as Jessie thinks the time's ripe, she'll tell you and the hands what's going on. Then we'll put our heads together and figure out what we need to do."

"Sure," the foreman said, nodding. "That's the way it's always worked before, and we ain't lost too many times. Nor too many head of cattle, either."

With a departing nod to Ki, Wright walked away, heading for the bunkhouse, and Ki continued to the main house. In spite of his assurances to the foreman, he was not easy in his mind. Only rarely did he and

Jessie go separate ways, and he'd lost track of the number of times in the past when they'd narrowly escaped disaster by doing so.

Inside the main house Ki felt Jessie's absence even more keenly. To give himself something to do, he went to the battered rolltop desk that had belonged to Alex and took out the thick file containing the financial records of the Silver City mine. Spreading the reports on the desktop, Ki began tracing the mine's silver production records, its income and operating costs, and entering the totals for each year in neat columns that would make comparisons easy.

After he'd jotted down the figures and studied them for a few minutes, Ki began to frown as he saw the results that could be deduced from the neat columns of numbers. For the first three of the seven years after Bob Jernigan had been promoted to manager, the mine's annual production of smelted silver varied by only a half-dozen troy ounces. However, for the next four years the production showed significant variations.

During the first years after Jernigan's promotion, the quantity of silver ore produced and the costs of operation remained at much the same level. In the years that followed, either the mine's operating costs increased or the yield of pure silver from ore processing dropped, and the result of either was a decline in the net profit.

Ki had encountered a similar pattern of fluctuations twice before. They'd occurred in reports which he'd been scanning for Alex Starbuck during his early years of service as Alex's confidential aide. After he'd discovered the first set of variations and reported them to Jessie's father, Alex had shaken his head sadly.

"It's not too unusual," Alex had said. "Envy is a sad emotion for a man to feel." When he'd seen the puzzled look on Ki's face, Alex had gone on to explain, "Envy's at the root of all theft, Ki. When a man sees his employer making a profit through enterprise and investment, he becomes envious. He feels that he's entitled to the same share taken by the man who hired him. If the employee's honest, he'll ask for a raise. If he's too weak to do that, he'll begin stealing."

Ki's reminiscences ended abruptly when the silence of the big room was broken by the chiming of the grandfather clock which stood in one corner. As the clear tuneful notes continued, he looked at the clock and was surprised to see that both its hands were pointing upward at the midnight hour. With a small frown forming on his usually impassive face, Ki pushed the pages of figures aside and walked to the front door.

There were no lights shining from the windows of the bunkhouse, none from the kitchen or mess hall. Only the glimmer of lamplight spilling down the hall from the room where he'd been working broke the darkness. Ki's small frown deepened for a moment, then his face cleared as he told himself that Jessie and Walters must have ridden farther than they'd planned and that when nightfall overtook them they'd decided to stop at the nearest line shack rather than ride back through the darkness.

Although a nagging wisp of worry continued to rankle in his mind, Ki closed the door. He started for the study where he'd been working, intending to blow out the lamps, but before he'd taken two steps, he decided to leave them burning in the event Jessie returned before daybreak. Then he climbed the stairs to his own room and went to bed.

"I don't intend to give you an excuse for killing me," Jessie said calmly as Walters continued to press the cold steel muzzle of his pistol into her neck. "And if you've got ideas about holding me for ransom, I'll be very glad to send a message to Ki, authorizing him to pay you any reasonable amount to release me unharmed."

"Now, that's real interesting, Miss Starbuck. It makes me feel better already," Walters told her. "But I ain't fool enough to send back any word just yet. We're still too close to that main house of yours."

"If you send a message to Ki right away, unless you have some kind of wild idea about the size of the ransom I'm sure you're going to demand to release me, you can have the money and be on your way as soon as you're paid."

Walters's response was between a snort of disbelief and a guffaw. When he'd caught his breath after his explosive laugh he said, "Oh, sure. And I'd just bet a pretty penny that if I was to send back word about what I figure to get paid for letting you go free, I'd have your chink and them ranch hands after me before I could count to ten."

"Not if I told them to leave you alone," Jessie responded quickly. "And I'm perfectly willing to tell them not to go after you in return for you releasing me unharmed right now."

"So you say," Walters retorted.

"My men will do just what I tell them to," Jessie assured him. "And if you'll do what I've just suggested, we'll both save a lot of time and trouble."

"Now, the last thing in the world I'd be likely to do is what you've just suggested. And there's something else you might as well know first crack out of the box."

Jessie frowned. "What's that?"

"I don't aim to pay any mind when you try to sweet-talk me. From what I've seen of you the little time I've been here, you're real good at that."

"How could I talk you—" Jessie began.

"You're trying it right now!" Walters broke in.

Jessie persisted. She started to repeat her question. "Now, how could I say anything that would—"

Before she could finish what she was starting to say, Walters cut her short. "Just close your mouth right now and keep it closed. We been sitting here jabbering too long as it is. We got a good bit of ground to cover before it gets too dark."

"You've been planning this for quite a while, haven't you?" Jessie asked Walters.

"You'd be real surprised if I told you how long, Miss Starbuck," he answered. "And I sure ain't going to let nothing happen that'd give you a chance to upset me. Like you making a grab for that Colt in your holster. Just stay real still while I get it from you."

Standing up in his stirrups, Walters leaned to grasp the butt of Jessie's revolver and slide it from her holster. He kept his own pistol muzzle pushed firmly to her neck as he moved, and did not ease the pressure until he'd dropped her Colt into his saddlebag.

"We'll move along now," he told her. "It's going to take us a good spell to get where we're going."

Jessie made a final effort to persuade Walters to change his plans. She said, "We'll both save time and trouble if you'll just listen to me. All I'm saying is—"

"You've said enough already!" Walters snapped. "Just hush up while I finish my job!"

As Walters spoke he was reaching for the cluster of thin leather strips that dangled from one of his saddle rings. Jessie watched him in stolid silence, but he kept his pistol's muzzle trained on her while he pulled out a pair of the strips. She'd expected him to tie her hands, and had decided that if she resisted him she'd only provoke him further. She made up her mind instantly to do as she'd done before when taken captive by an enemy, to make no move unless she was sure it would succeed.

Though the pressure the fake ranger put on the strips of leather as he lashed Jessie's hands to the horn of her saddle caused the thin rough strips of rawhide to cut into her wrists with a painful pressure, she did not argue or tighten her muscles or offer any kind of resistance.

"Now, then," Walters said as he inspected Jessie's bonds. "We'll move on, and if you know what's good for you, you won't start giving me any trouble."

"Do you mind telling me where we're going?"

"You'll find out soon enough. I've put in a lot of time getting everything all planned out. There's a place up ahead that I fixed up for a hidey-hole."

"I hope we don't have far to go," Jessie told him. "You've tied these saddle strings far too tight for comfort. And I'd hate to have my arms pulled out of their sockets if this horse should make a misstep and throw me. At least give me a little play so I can be sure of staying in my saddle."

Walters was busy now disentangling the reins of Jessie's mount and freeing the leathers from the rawhide strips he'd used to bind her wrists. He got the reins free and bent forward to inspect her bound-up wrists.

"You're not hurting as far as I can tell, but I guess I better oblige you. We've got a pretty good ways to go, and if I don't, you'll be yattering at me all the time."

Moving with a haste that betrayed his impatience to start, Walters removed the leather strips, retied Jessie's wrists, and secured them to the horn of her saddle with a separate string.

"I hope that satisfies you," he went on as he finished the last knot and tested it with hard jerk. "If it don't, you'll just have to put up with being a mite uncomfortable. I'm not fool enough to let you have any slack in these lashings around your wrists. Now shut up and settle down. I've got enough to think about without listening to a lot of your fool palaver."

Jessie recognized the tone of finality in his voice. She let her arms go slack while Walters finished freeing the reins of her horse. He pulled the leathers with him while he swung back into his own saddle, glanced at Jessie over his shoulder, and toed his horse into motion.

Ahead, less than a quarter of a mile from the point from which they were starting, the grass began to thin out. Instead of carpeting the earth in a waving unbroken blanket of green, it became patchy, the clumps of waving grass stems shorter. Still farther ahead even the patches of green showed more and more rarely, and in the distance the green patches vanished and only seamed, scarred, sunbaked soil was visible to the edge of the horizon.

Jessie knew that she had very little time to lose. She dropped her hands to the saddle horn and began working on the knot with her fingers, trying to create a bit of slack. The narrow strips of rawhide began stretching slowly, but they did yield. Jessie twisted her hands vigorously, pulling her arms taut by leaning as far back in the saddle as she could, and after she'd repeated the maneuver several times she felt the lashing begin to go a bit slack.

Hoping she'd stretched the plaint rawhide enough, Jessie tried to slip the looped thong over the knob atop the saddle horn. The pliant leather saddle strings yielded slowly, but at last she managed to pull the loop free. Now she could raise her arms, and that was all that she needed to carry out her plan.

Keeping her eyes fixed on Walters, hoping that he would not turn suddenly to look at her, Jessie reached up to the crown of her broad-brimmed Stetson. She turned her head as she ran her fingers along its narrow band of corded silk ribbon until they encountered the band's decorative bow, and she could feel the smooth metal of her good-luck pin which adorned the ribbon.

One of Alex's many gifts to Jessie before his untimely death had been the pin which she was now fingering. It was a simple gold and silver brooch, with the circles of gold at each end interlocking the single silver loop in the center. The round strips of metal were only a bit larger in diameter than a woman's narrow wedding ring. Encouraged by her success so far, Jessie bent her head sideways and fingered the pin until she managed to free it from the hatband.

Jessie had worn the pin as a hat ornament from the day Alex had given it to her. As much as she disliked parting with it now, it was the only object she had that she was sure would be heavy enough to throw and be visible in the dwindling patches of

73

shortgrass. She glanced at Walters again, just in time to see him starting to turn in his saddle and look back at her. She quickly dropped her hands to the saddlehorn and grasped it, closing her hands to hide the brooch.

When Walters glanced back over his shoulder, he saw Jessie sitting erect and motionless in the saddle, her hands clasped around the horn in the position she'd been forced to keep them in because of her bonds. His inspection was brief and cursory. As soon as he turned to look ahead once more, Jessie quickly flipped the brooch toward the clump of thin prairie grass that she'd selected.

To her dismay the glittering brooch fell short of the grass clump. It landed on the hard-baked ground a few inches away from the thin shoots of green. Jessie looked at Walters, and breathed a small sigh of relief when she saw that his eyes were still fixed on the landscape ahead. As best she could, she slid her hand back into the loose loops of the rawhide thongs that had been binding both her hands to the saddle horn.

She flexed her arms a time or two, and succeeded in drawing the thong to the saddle horn a bit tighter, hoping that when the time came for Walters to release her he would fail to notice how loose the disturbed knot really was. Then she set her gaze on the broken country that stretched ahead. When Walters turned back to look at her the next time, she was staring poker-faced at the horizon.

Ki woke with a start. He saw that the windows of his room were gray and brightening slowly as the before-sunrise dimness began its steady advance westward in lightening the sky. Rolling out of bed, he slid into his customary daytime wear, a *cache-sex* under loose black trousers and a light jacket with wide wrist-length sleeves. He slipped his feet into the sandals lying beside his bed and went down the hall to Jessie's bedroom.

A light tap with his fingertips brought no response. Ki knocked again, this time with his calloused knuckles, and when Jessie's voice did not respond, he opened the door and peered inside, knowing in advance what he would see. The room was empty, Jessie's bed undisturbed.

His face more than usually sober, Ki went back to his own room long enough to strap onto his forearm the leather case containing his *shuriken*. He stepped to the corner nearest the head of his bed and picked up his Winchester in its saddle scabbard, then made a cursory tour of the empty house to be sure everything was in order.

Opening the front door, he saw that as he'd expected, lamplight glowed from the mess-hall windows. As Ki walked across the short expanse of well-beaten earth between the main house and the mess hall, his mind was probing the events of the previous day, trying to think of some reason why Jessie had not returned.

He'd last seen Jessie at the corrals, where he'd known she was most likely to be, checking on the condition of Sun's sore hoof. After he'd delivered Walters's note to her the only thing she'd mentioned concerning her plans for the day was that she and Walters would be riding across the southeastern part of the Circle Star in order for her to show him how the land lay in that direction.

Jessie had made no mention of the exact spots she intended to visit, nor had she given Ki any clue as to when she and Walters would return. Though Ki kept assuring himself that nothing could have happened to Jessie and Walters, the news that their unexpected guest had brought kept recurring to Ki's mind. He'd begun to wonder if the gang of rustlers the Texas Ranger had described might not have arrived sooner than expected.

"Well, now! Look at what the cat dragged in!" Gimpy, the lame cook, exclaimed when he looked up from the huge dishpan in which he was stirring pancake batter and saw Ki entering the kitchen. "You figure on having breakfast with the hands instead of waiting for Miss Jessie?"

"I'm not thinking about breakfast right now," Ki replied. "Jessie didn't come back last night, and I'm concerned about her. I'm sure that if she'd come in, you'd've heard her, your room being right here across from the main house."

"If she come in, I sure didn't hear her," Gimpy said, frowning. "And you know how light I sleep."

"That's why I came over to ask you," Ki said. "I wake up pretty easily myself, but I might not've heard her, with that heavy carpet in the hall over there."

"Likely something happened to her horse," Gimpy suggested. "Or the horse that stranger was riding."

Ki shook his head. "No. There's not a chance in a hundred that something could've happened to both of their horses. Even if both her horse and the ranger's had been lamed, they'd've had time between dark and daylight to walk back here."

"Well, you got me believing something's wrong now," Gimpy said. "I guess you got the right hunch about going looking for 'em."

"Did Jessie get any victuals from you before they left?"

"A sandwich apiece for her and that stranger, in case they run late getting back. I reckon you're going out looking for 'em?"

"Of course," Ki replied. "But if they've been caught out on the range overnight, they'll be bear-hungry. Have you got any kind of victuals I can take in my saddlebag?"

"I got some pieces of leftover steak from supper that I can put up in sandwiches for you."

"Good. Start fixing them up, and I'll go get my horse saddled. Put them in a saltsack or something, and I'll pick them up before I leave."

"How about you, Ki? You ain't had breakfast, and if—"

"Make me a sandwich, Gimpy. I'll eat it as I ride," Ki replied as he started for the door.

He hurried to the corral and saddled the long-winded pinto he favored. Guiding the horse back to the mess hall, he found Gimpy waiting outside the door. He took the sandwich the cook offered him and waited while Gimpy tucked the bundle of food in his saddlebag. Then Ki reined around and rode into the beginning sunrise, heading for the eastern boundary of the Circle Star.

★

# Chapter 7

Jessie had no way of knowing exactly how long she and Walters had been moving steadily across the baren expanse of rough sunbaked brownish-yellow earth. With the fast-scudding clouds covering most of the sky now, it was impossible to judge exactly how many hours of daylight remained, but Jessie guessed that at most only two or three hours would bring darkness. This would mean that between three and four hours had passed since he'd made her his prisoner and taken her across the fence line that marked the Circle Star's eastern boundary.

It was obvious that Walters had a destination in mind, and Jessie was more than ever thankful that she'd tossed her hat ornament on the ground before her captor had led her through the gap where he'd cut the Circle Star's boundary fence.

Jessie was angry with herself because of her failure to recognize Walters as a fake when he'd first shown up at the ranch. Her anger had almost burst the bonds of self-restraint when she saw the sagging barbed wire strands of the boundary fence, but she knew that an outburst from her would do no good and might harm her chances of making an escape later.

She'd held her temper in check when she saw the twin strands of barbed wire drooping to the ground. She watched in poker-faced silence while the fake ranger took fence-pliers from his saddle bag and made a quick job of stretching the wire taut and twisting its ends together again. As soon as Walters had completed his job of fence repairs, they'd started moving east, following the almost-invisible traces of the trail over which cattle had been driven to the Rio Grande in the beginning days of the big Texas ranches.

Unused for many years, the trail had almost disappeared under the ravages of time and weather. Now they were still following its faint vestiges, and it was obvious to Jessie that Walters was much more familiar with the terrain than she'd imagined him to be when they started out. After they'd covered the first few miles, where the ground was relatively soft, traces of the long-unused trail began to fade. Now it was visible only at long intervals and in short stretches on the hard reddish sunbaked soil. A half-dozen miles back they'd left the reasonably level country where the reddish soil was dotted by stretches of feebly surviving grass and had entered the beginning of the *malpais* which still stretched ahead of them.

As far as Jessie could see, the badlands were unbroken, an expanse of barren boulder-studded broken earth. The ground was almost bare of any vegetation except for a few struggling mesquite clumps and an occasional small patch of yellow-tipped shortgrass, obviously struggling to survive in the arid yellowish soil. Here and there small outcrops of rock ledges showed just above the level of the earth, and at rare intervals she could see a cluster of a few large boulders perched precariously on a ledge, or the stone-tipped humps that marked similar boulders still buried in the earth.

As nearly as Jessie could observe, the trace Walters was following had seen virtually no recent use. It was so lightly marked that most of the time she was forced to slit her eyes when looking ahead in order to pick up its course. She'd seen no clearly defined hoofprints on it, and even when she glanced over her shoulder at the area, they'd just left she was barely able to make out the hoofprints that their horses left on the gravely rock-studded earth.

Whenever she concentrated on looking ahead, Jessie could see no change in the landscape. The rocky terrain extended to the jagged line of the eastern horizon. Looking back, she saw that the clouds which were just beginning to look threatening when they began now covered the sky and were moving in the same direction that Walters was leading her. The semidesert they were crossing had a sameness which offered few landmarks that could be used to guide them, but she'd noticed that even in the short time they'd been moving after leaving the Circle Star's line fence, Walters had changed their direction more than once.

With no sun to guide her, no shadows on the ground by which to judge the time, and in country which had become less and less familiar to her after they'd left the circle Star's boundary fence, Jessie's frustration continued to mount. She searched her memory for clues that might have been lodged in it from the maps she'd looked at, but found herself frustrated by the lack of any clues.

As best she could remember from the maps at which she'd glanced now and then, if they kept on their present course it would take them across the broad swathe of badly broken country that stretched between the Davis Mountains and the Rio Grande.

If Walters had any reason for veering at so many angles, she could only attribute it to his unfamiliarity with the country they were crossing, for the terrain looked much the same in all directions. All that she could really be sure of was that long ago they'd turned away from the faint vestiges of the trail left by the few herds of steers that had been driven to the Mexican market years in the past. She'd seen no evidence of any other trail which would account for her captor's choice of their route.

"I do hope you know where you're taking me," she called to Walters as their horses slowed while ascending a long upslope.

"That's not for you to worry about," Walters replied.

"You're the one who should be worrying," Jessie told him, her voice tart. "My hands back on the Circle Star know this country better than you do, I'm sure. So does Ki. How long do you think it's going to take them to pick up our trail?"

Twisting in his saddle to face her, Walters went on, "They won't miss you till it's too dark for 'em to start looking for you tonight. Why do you figure I was asking you so many questions about how the land lays ahead of us? I know what's ahead of us better than you or your hands do. We'll be safe in my hideout a long time before they even start. And you'll know where we're heading for when I pull up and get off my horse."

"There's no real reason why you shouldn't tell me," she pointed out. "I don't see anybody around that I could tell your secret to."

"I aim to keep it that way, too," he told her. "You'll just have to wait and find out for yourself."

"How long will that be?"

"Like I just got through saying, you'll know when we get there. And I don't intend to waste time, because from the look of that sky behind us, there's a pretty good-sized storm chasing after us right now."

Twisting in her saddle, Jessie looked back. The aspect of the sky had changed radically since they'd started. Now there was no gap of blue sky between them and the ominous clouds rolling in their direction. The dark thunderheads were directly overhead and moving fast. Even as she was turning her head away, a bolt of lightning zigzagged from them, and a low mutter of thunder rumbled in the distance.

"I guess you can see for yourself what I was talking about," Walters told her. Then, with a tone of finality in his voice, he added, "Now you've got as much chatter as you're going to get out of me. Just keep your mouth shut and keep riding."

Jessie fell silent, and turned her thoughts toward figuring out a way of getting free.

Ki pulled up his mount when in the distance he could see the twin barbwire strands that marked the eastern boundary of the Circle Star. For several minutes he sat in his saddle studying the terrain. The eastern areas of the big spread were the least-used of the ranch's several principal ranges. They were not only the farthest from the main house, but had the least desirable graze.

Here the ground would support only shortgrass, which tended to grow in patches on the thin layer of soil that covered the underlying strata of limestone and schist. The grass cover that had begun thinning a quarter of a mile just inside the fence was patchier now. Beyond the fence line, where the *mailpais* began to take over the landscape, the patches of grass were even smaller and the patches thinner. In many places the jagged edges of limestone outcrops replaced the thinning grass.

Ki reined in a short distance from the boundary fence in order to be able to look along it as far as possible in both directions. The taut metal strands that stretched gleaming to the each horizon showed no sagging areas, no breaks. Even when Ki stood up in his stirrups to extend the range of his vision, he could see no evidence of sagging wire nor could he see any sign that Jessie and Walters had been in the vicinity.

He was settling down into his saddle again when an alien glitter on the ground caught his eyes. Ki twitched the reins of his horse to turn it into the direction of the gleam he'd glimpsed. Even before he reached the glistening object, he'd recognized it as the brooch which Jessie wore as a hat ornament. A frown formed on Ki's usually impassive face when he swung to the ground and picked up the pin.

"This didn't fall off by accident," he said aloud. In the still air of the prairie his low thoughtful murmur sounded like a shout. "And Jessie wouldn't part with it unless she had a good reason. She dropped it here because—"

Ki stopped short, his eyes turning toward the

fence. The silvery strands of barbwire seemed intact at first glance. Then beyond the next post he saw the bulging spots in the barbed wire where it had been spliced. He stepped up to the fence and inspected the splices.

They told him nothing that he had already deduced. The break in the barbed wire had been made with bare hands, not fence pliers, nor were pliers among the items Ki carried in his saddlebags. However, his muscular hands were strong and deft and his fingers callused. Ki made quick work of parting the barbed wire strands and led his horse through the gap he'd created.

He twisted the strands together, and though he was in a hurry to follow the faint tracks that led away from the fence, he did not mount his horse until he'd dropped to his knees and a made a close inspection of the ground around the break in the barbed wire.

Though the hoofprints on the hard-baked ground beyond the fence were shallow and often indistinct, Ki knew that each hoof of each horse shod by a blacksmith required a slightly different contour and size of shoe. He was confident when he'd finished his scrutiny that he could identify each of the eight shoes worn by the horses which Jessie and Walters were riding. Then he wasted no more time, but mounted and set out to follow the faint prints that led away from the line fence.

Darkness and the storm at last caught up with Jessie and Walters. The first big drops of rain were falling and the shimmering sheen below the black clouds were above them now. The jagged horizon line behind them was too black for Jessie to make out any of its details when Walters turned his horse aside and

Jessie saw a short stretch of soft sandy soil between them and the gaping black triangle that broke the canyon's walls.

Abruptly the crunching of hard stony soil under the horses' hooves ended. They moved in hushed silence; only the soft whisper of hooves being planted on soft sand was audible. The western horizon line was no longer visible, and in the east only a thin slit of blue showed between the bottom line of the clouds and the rims of the canyon.

Walters rode on through the triangular opening and into the cave. Jessie peered through its darkness and could see only the vaguest outline of the cavern's walls. Then Walters reined in, and Jessie's horse stopped behind his.

"I guess you'll be glad as I am to get outa that saddle," Walters said after he'd dismounted and was stepping up to the led-horse Jessie was riding.

"I'd be even more relieved if I had some idea of what you've got in mind," Jessie replied.

"If I told you that, you'd know as much as I do," Walters said, fumbling in the dark at the rawhide strings that bound her wrists to her saddle horn.

"Are we just stopping here for the night?"

"All you need to know is that we've stopped," Walters answered as he finally fumbled the knots free. "And I don't figure you'll be fool enough to try to get away, not knowing where we are and not having a gun and all like that."

Jessie did not reply. Walters finished pulling the saddle strings away from her wrists and stepped back.

"All right," he went on. "You can get off that nag now. But don't try no fool stunts, like making a getaway. I'd hate to have to shoot you, after all the trouble I took bringing you here."

"I'd be just as happy if you hadn't bothered," Jessie told him as she slid from her saddle. Her legs cramped a bit as she took a step or two, but she ignored the small pain. When she went on, her voice was as cool and unworried as though she was refusing an invitation to have a cup of tea. "But now that I'm here, I'm a bit curious to know what you have in mind."

"Why, I figured a lady as smart as you are would've tumbled to that a long time ago," Walters said. "But let's put that to one side for a minute. I got to get everything fixed up so you'll be comfortable while we're waiting out that storm."

Although a half-dozen questions popped full-blown into Jessie's mind, she voiced none of them. Instead, she turned to inspect the cavern. If the darkness of the oncoming clouds outside had been black, the interior of the cave was even blacker. The burst of flame from the match Walters struck on his boot-sole blinded her for a moment, just as a lightning flash would have done outside.

For a few moments Jessie blinked while her eyes were adjusting to the light. By the time the moisture that filled them and started her involuntarily blinking had cleared away, the light had settled down to a steady yellowish glow, and Jessie looked around, taking stock of her new surroundings.

Though only the area near the small still-struggling fire was really visible, Jessie could see at a glance that the cave was very large indeed. Its top was a dozen feet above her head, its walls at least twenty feet apart, and she had no way of knowing how far back it extended, for the fire lighted an area no more than a few paces from the entrance.

"I don't know how far back it stretches," Walters

volunteered when he saw Jessie peering into the blackness. "Never had the time to follow this place in more'n about twenty feet from here. It's a big one, though. You ain't going to be cramped for room while you're here. And that's going to be till your Chinaman back at that fancy ranch comes up with a big chunk of money."

"I see," Jessie said. "You intend to keep me a prisoner here while you collect this ransom you're expecting to get?"

"You called the turn on the first card out of the box," Walters agreed. "We figured it'd be worth a whole big pile of money for you to walk out of here alive."

"And how do you expect Ki to get whatever ransom money you're asking for?"

"Well, now," Walters replied. "That's for you to fix up. But you ought not have too much trouble doing it. Most rich folks like you has got big chunks of cash money stashed away where they can get to it quick and easy."

"I'm afraid you're mistaken about that," Jessie told him. "I don't keep a great deal of cash at the ranch, just enough to meet the payroll and cover running expenses for a couple of months."

"Why, everybody knows you got more money than most folks can even think about, Miss Starbuck. Me and my friends aim to get a pretty good chunk of it a lot quicker and easier than we could make as much selling even rustled cattle that didn't cost us nothing but the trouble to drive 'em to market."

"And how long do you think it will take for me to get the amount of cash that you're obviously going to want?" As she posed the question Jessie's voice was as cool and unruffled as if she were asking him for a cup of tea.

"That don't make much never-mind to me and my friends, Miss Starbuck. We'll wait just as long as it takes."

"A month? Three months? Six months?" she prodded.

"Oh, you'll figure a way to get the cash before then," Walters said confidently.

"What makes you think that?"

Walters's voice hardened and an expression which Jessie had never seen on his face before formed as he replied, "Don't make no mistakes about me and my friends, Miss Starbuck. Now, paying us money won't hurt you even a little bit, you got so much of it. But all your money can't buy fingers and toes or a new nose. And some of my friends is likely to get hard up for a woman if we've got to wait too long to get the cash we're after. They'll be hard to stop when—"

"Never mind finishing your threats," Jessie broke in. "I understand quite well what you're hinting."

"I sorta figured you might," he said, nodding. "Now, suppose you stop stalling and let's us get down to cases."

"I take that to mean you're ready to tell me how much you want and how it's to be delivered?"

"Something like that. Or at least, if you say we're seeing eye to eye, we can have a bite to eat first, and then talk business."

Jessie had no illusions about Walters's threats. She was sure he was quite prepared to carry them out, if given enough time. However, while she was purposely dragging out their verbal sparring match, she'd decided that her best bet was to be reasonably amenable, to stall as long as Walters would allow her to do so, and to fight fire with fire by being as deceptive as he'd been.

"I don't suppose I really have a great deal of choice," she told Walters.

"No. I wouldn't say you have, either," he agreed.

"I'm sure you'll understand that I'm going to need time to do a bit of thinking about your demands," she went on. "So far all you've told me is that you're going to ask for a great deal of money to release me. The first thing I'll need to know is how much you're thinking of asking in ransom."

For a moment Walters hesitated, his face twisted in a frown of concentration. At last he said aggressively, "Not a dime less than half a million dollars."

Jessie did not reply at once. The amount Walters was asking for did not disturb her, in fact she'd half-expected that his demand would be for twice that much. Walters had not taken his eyes off Jessie's face since he'd stated his ransom figure, and she'd been careful to show no surprise or other emotion.

"That's a great deal of money," Jessie said when she decided she'd stretched to a limit the time her captor would allow her to take before replying.

"It ain't much to you," he answered. "Why, everybody in the country knows how rich you are."

"Just as I told you a minute ago, being what you call rich doesn't mean I've got that much loose cash lying around."

"If you ain't got it in hand, you can get it pretty quick, I'd imagine."

"Perhaps not as fast or as easily as you seem to believe. I'll need to do some thinking before I give you an answer."

"Now, look here, Miss Starbuck, you and me both

knows what your answer's got to be if you aim to get us to turn you loose."

"I think you realize that you've already had your answer," Jessie told him. "After all, you've got me in situation where I don't really have much choice."

"I sorta figured you'd look at it that way after you'd studied it over a bit," Walters said, nodding. "But I want you to dot the *i* 's and cross the *t* 's. Have we got a deal, or haven't we?"

"Oh, we've got a deal," Jessie agreed. "But I'm going to need some time."

"How much time?"

"That's what I still have to figure out," Jessie said with a frown. "Now I'm going to need to decide where and how I can get together a half-million dollars in cash."

"You still ain't said how long it's going to take you."

"Of course I haven't!" Jessie exclaimed. "You can't expect me to do that in ten minutes, as tired as I am after the kind of day you've dragged me through. Right at this minute, all I can think of is getting some sleep. Whether you like it or not, you're going to have to wait until tomorrow before we do any more talking."

Walters did not reply at once. He frowned thoughtfully for a few moments, then said, "All right. You can sleep a while. But don't try to pull any fancy tricks, like trying to get away. Because if you do, I'm apt to forget how much you're worth on the hoof to me and my friends and put a bullet through your head."

★

# Chapter 8

When he left the line fence to follow the trail of hoofprints that led away from the Circle Star, Ki was reasonably sure that he'd been correct in the deductions he'd made regarding their origin. As the faint half-circles that were pressed into the soil led him farther from the fence, doubts began to plague him. Afterthoughts started drifting into his mind, telling him that he had no absolute certainty his assumptions were as valid as he'd first assumed. He realized only too well that the margin of error allowed him was very slim indeed, but he also understood that in order to establish the facts he must follow the only lead he had.

Ki continued his slow but steady progress, moving toward the southeast, away from the line fence. He watched the long-unused trail carefully, looking for signs which would confirm his belief that the last riders who'd passed over it had indeed been Jessie and Walters.

There was very little for Ki to go by because of

the nature of the terrain. On the stretches where grass and weeds had found the ground hospitable to their roots and where the sandy soil was firm enough to hold its shape, he had little trouble following the faint impressions. However, each time they vanished on some stretch of rock or strip of gravel, his nagging uncertainty returned to bother him.

As he rode farther into the wide canyon, Ki's job became more difficult. Here there was less vegetation and the bottom of the deep cleft was more rock-strewn sand than firm soil. In the loose sand the prints he was tracking did not hold their shape, and where they were more clearly defined in a rare stretch of almost solid earth, weeds and grasses had overgrown the dim trail. Even in the occasional strips where the soil was firm enough to pack, weeds had rooted, and if Ki did find tracks on the firmer ground the occasional outlines of a horse's hoof had almost always been blurred by the movements of the plants when they straightened up after being crushed.

Between the stretches of parched, loose sandy soil that dominated the land through which the trail ran, Ki crossed many spots where stones alone formed its floor. In some of these places he could see at a glance the clear signs that the loosely embedded rocks had been disturbed recently. However, the stone-covered stretches did not retain hoofprints as did the loose dry soil. At times Ki had difficulty in determining whether the prints were old or new and whether they'd been made by one horse or two.

Though he stopped at each expanse that was fairly free from stones, Ki encountered very few such stretches of reasonably firm soil that contained neither weeds nor stones. There was no place where the hoofprints were clearly enough outlined and defined to allow him to compare them readily with those he'd locked into his memory at the spot where he'd left the Circle Star's range.

Some distance ahead of him, Ki could see that the distance between the walls of the wide valley through which he was traveling were converging, that the valley was growing narrower. For a moment he considered mounting to one rim and watching its floor from the advantage height would give him. Then almost as quickly as he'd conceived the idea, he abandoned it, because of the difficulty he might encounter in returning to the floor quickly if that move became necessary.

Far sooner than he'd anticipated, the valley became nothing more than a narrow arroyo in which stones lined the floor as well as the walls. Reasonably certain that in such rocky stretches he'd find nothing that he hadn't encountered before, Ki decided to hurry, and to pay only enough attention to the tracks he'd set out to follow to be sure that Jessie and her abductor were still ahead. He touched the flank of his horse with his heel and the animal began moving faster.

Because he'd been concentrating on the trail, Ki had paid little attention to the sky. The first indication he had that one of the region's sudden storms was brewing was a distant rumble of thunder behind him. Its broken muttering sounded like a giant's throat-clearing cough. He looked at the sky when the rumblings began and and saw behind him the ominous black clouds that had already swallowed the sun's bright rays at an alarming speed as they swept toward him above the broken terrain.

Standing up in his stirrups to increase the area he would be able to scan, Ki saw behind him a sparkling sheet of glistening raindrops. They formed a scintillating curtain that looked as solid as an unbroken wall of glass filling the space between the clouds and the earth. On both sides of the wide ravine small puffs of earth were spurting up where the heaviest rain was falling.

Automatically, Ki reached behind him to get his slicker. His hand encountered nothing but saddle leather and he remembered belatedly that because of the hurry in which he'd left the Circle Star he'd neglected to lash his slicker into its usual position on the rear saddle skirt. Philosophically, but with a small grimace, he accepted the prospect that he'd be soaked soon after the first raindrops reached him.

Pushed eastward by a brisk breeze the big raindrops that soon began gushing from the now-leaden sky started pelting him. Ki's loosely fitting black jacket was soaked quickly, and so were his trousers. The steadily falling rain seeped between his buttocks and his saddle and the legs of his trousers no longer flapped loosely but clung to his calves like chilling leggins. His discomfort was increased by the constant dripping of rainwater from his thick shock of shoulder-length black hair.

Riding in the position which most cowhands on the far West Texas range had learned to take when traveling through a storm, Ki bent forward in the saddle, his head down and his shoulders hunched. Only a few minutes passed after the full blast of the rainstorm reached him before water started creeping along his shoulders and down his arms. The drops flowed over his hand and wet the reins, turning their leather into slippery hard-to-hold strips.

Though Ki tried to disregard the rain as a minor nuisance, he could not banish totally the effect of the small icy trickles that flowed along his neck, oozed inside his blouse along his spine, and turned his saddle into a small chilly puddle. At the same time other trickles were creeping along his shoulders and down his arms, wetting the reins and making them slippery in his hands.

Hunched in the saddle, Ki let his cow pony have its head and pick its own way through the downpour, which showed no signs of diminishing. If anything, the gloom was growing deeper, the clouds so heavy now and the rain pelting in such big thick drops that the canyon had an atmosphere of late twilight. He knew that he had only two choices. One was to stop in the first place that offered some kind of shelter. So far, Ki had seen no such spot. The second choice was to keep moving and hope that Walters had chosen to stop somewhere ahead and wait out the end of the rainstorm.

Neither option appealed to him, but without shelter stopping made no sense and his increasing worry about Jessie kept him pushing steadily ahead. Without the sun by which he could judge time, and with the storm clouds turning the usually bright day into as perpetual dusk, Ki lost track of time as his horse plodded ahead.

Peering through the veil of raindrops, looking for any sign which might indicate Jessie's passage, trying to convince himself that perhaps he might even find her in some sheltered spot ahead, Ki noticed that the canyon walls were beginning to squeeze together. He'd covered perhaps another half-mile when he was sure he glimpsed a hint of motion through the blurring downfall. Before he could shake away the big drops that were rolling from his headband into his eyes and blurring his vision, a shot rang out and muzzle-blast spurted in a crimson streak that was almost invisible through the blinding downpour.

As the slug whistled angrily past Ki's head, he threw himself sideways from his saddle. Even though he was toppling he managed to slide a *shuriken* from the leather case strapped on his forearm. When he landed with a splash on the puddled ground, Ki had the wicked throwing blade in his hand, ready to send it spinning toward his attacker as soon as the sniper became visible.

Ki's horse had stopped a moment after he'd dropped from the saddle. Looking beyond the animal he saw a vague slicker-shrouded form approaching through the pelting raindrops. The only thing he could see clearly was the rifle in the hands of the oncoming figure.

Straining his eyes as he sprawled on the muddy trail, Ki saw at once that neither his position nor his rain-diminished vision favored a *shuriken* attack until his target had come closer. Holding the razor-edged blade ready, Ki waited.

Jessie woke, and as always she was alert the moment her eyes opened. Without moving she glanced around the cave. The glow of red coals near the opposite side of the cavern did little to dispel the black gloom that shrouded its interior. All that she could see was the motionless figure of Harry Walters. He was sitting on the floor of the cave on the other side of what remained of the fire, leaning against the sheer wall of the big cavern, looking at her across the dying blaze.

"Well, now, Miss Starbuck," he said. "You've had a pretty good sleep, and we got the first part of our deal all wound up proper before you dozed off, so

I'd say it's time now for us to work out the rest of it."

"I don't see how you can be much help in doing that," Jessie replied. "I certainly don't intend to discuss such things as my bank accounts—or any of my other private financial affairs—with you."

"Don't start hollering before you're hurt, ma'am," Walters shot back. "I guess you're so used to being the big high muckety-muck that you ain't really tumbled yet to what you're up against."

"I understand quite well that I'm your prisoner," she told him. "And I hope you understand a few things, too."

"Such as?"

"You want my money, I want my freedom," Jessie went on. "I don't especially want to give you any money, and I don't suppose you'd want to kill me if I refused. If you did kill me, you'd never get anything except the experience that other outlaws and killers have had before you, dangling at the end of a hangman's rope."

"Somebody'd sure have to catch up with me first, before that happened."

"You can be sure that somebody would."

"Now, look here, Miss Starbuck, all you've said so far is either an *if* or a *maybe*. From the way you talk, I got a feeling that what you're trying to do is spook me into letting you go."

"You might be closer to the fact if you said that what I'm doing is trying to keep you from getting into a great deal more trouble than you're in right now," Jessie countered.

"I been around long enough to know what trouble's like," Walters said with a shrug. "And I've stood for your stalling all I aim to. I'm going to bring you a tablet and a pencil that I've been carrying in my saddlebag, and you're going to write whatever it is you need to say to get me my ransom money. I don't much care what you put down, as long as it gets me my payoff."

All that Ki could see through the sudden spate of a fresh blinding downpour was a bulky shape draped from chin to ankles in a raincoat and holding a rifle aimed at him. The muzzle of the weapon was steady, and the gun's front sight only two or three yards away. The storm hat that his challenger had on shaded the other's face and hid its features.

Ki did not plan his attack beyond the first move. He concentrated his attention on the rifle's muzzle, and when the front sight was a yard away Ki launched a mae-geri-keage kick with the rifle's muzzle as his target. His foot landed squarely on the tip of the muzzle, and the rifle flew up, but as it rose the momentum of its motion jerked the gunstock and triggered off a shot.

Ki felt the breeze of the speeding bullet as it passed only an inch or so from his cheek, but by this time he was toppling backward, for the momentum of his rising leg had dislodged his already precarious footing on the thick coating of slick mud that now covered the trail's surface.

Even as he was falling, Ki's well-honed skill guided his moves almost instinctively. He began rolling to his feet in an effort to continue attacking, but his unknown assailant stepped forward and let the muzzle of the rifle drop. Ki felt the hard steel jammed into his midriff and stopped his effort before he'd gained the momentum that might have pushed the gun's barrel away. The pressure of the rifle muzzle did not diminish. Then his adversary spoke. To Ki's surprise, the voice was that of a woman.

"Now, just lay quiet and I won't have to pull the trigger," she said. "Hand over your gun, and I'll let you get up. I don't guess you'll dry out, but it'll be a mite more comfortable than laying there on the ground."

"I don't have a gun," Ki replied. "But I'd like to get up out of this mud puddle, all right."

"I wasn't born yesterday, mister whoever you are," she said. "If you're telling the truth, you're the first man I can remember seeing around here who don't travel heeled. Suppose you just roll over while I make sure you ain't lying."

Obediently Ki rolled to lie face-down. He felt the quick movement of a hand over his hips and thighs, then the pressure of the rifle muzzle vanished as his captor stepped backward, away from him.

"All right. You can get up," the woman said. Her voice was still rasping, but not as harsh as it had been a moment earlier.

Springing nimbly to his feet, Ki turned to face the woman who held the rifle. She was bringing the muzzle of the weapon up, to keep its threat alive, but she did not take her eyes off Ki as she moved.

"Well, I'll be double-dog damned," she gasped when she saw his face. "You're a Chinee!"

"Japanese," Ki corrected her.

A sudden fierce gust of wind howled through the canyon. "There ain't much sense in us standing here palavering in this kind of weather," she said. "I've got a shakedown place not too far off. You better come along with me. This blow's going to last a while, and I'm getting colder and wetter every minute."

"Thanks for your offer," Ki told her. "But I've got to be moving on, I want to catch up with—"

"I ain't inviting you," the woman broke in, raising the muzzle of her rifle to cover Ki again. Her voice was as hard as any Ki had ever heard coming from a human throat. "I'm telling you. Just start on past me along the path—or what's left of it. I'll tell you where to head, and you keep in mind that I got this Remington pointed right at you. I don't guess I need to tell you that I ain't afraid to use it. Now, get going!"

"Here you are," Walters said, handing Jessie the tablet and pencil he'd taken from his saddlebags. "I won't tell you what to write down, but I don't guess I need to. You know what I want, so if you expect to see that ranch of yours again, you'll do like I told you to."

Jessie took the writing materials and sat gazing at them for a moment, then began writing:

*Ki, it seems that I've been kidnapped. Walters is holding me for ransom. He's not a Texas Ranger, but an outlaw. I don't see any way to refuse him. I've agreed to pay him the $500,000 he demands. You can get my power of attorney from the safe and use it any way that's necessary to get the cash. I know it's going to take you two or three weeks to get that much money together, and I'm sure you will do what you must to get it as quickly as possible. Walters hasn't told me how he wants the money delivered, but I'll ask him to attach the instructions to this note. Jessie.*

100

Jessie scanned the letter quickly and extended the tablet to Walters. She said, "I don't think you'll object to anything I've written here. I didn't give Ki any detailed orders or instructions, but he'll know what to do."

"You sure put a lot of store by that chink," Walters commented after he'd scanned Jessie's message. "It'd be a cold day in hell before I'd trust anybody I know with that much money. Why, that slant-eyes could take this and get that half-million and skip out and you'd never hear from him again."

"Don't worry about that happening," Jessie said. "There've been many times when Ki's handled a lot more money than that, not only for me, but for my father."

"Well, you know him better'n I do," the fake ranger went on. "And I got it all worked out how he can pass it over to me."

"Oh, I was sure you had," Jessie said. "That's why I added the line about you sending your own note with instructions for delivering it. And I'm equally sure you've worked out a way to deliver the note to Ki."

"Sure." Walters had started for the mouth of the cave and spoke over his shoulder as he went on, "Soon as this damn rain lets up, we'll be moving along. We ain't too far from where I got somebody waiting to take care of doing just that." He'd reached the mouth of the cavern and was gazing outside. "But we'll be here till the weather turns. It's still pouring down pretty heavy out there, and I'd a sight rather ride dry than wet. We'll bide our time and stay here till the rain passes over, so make yourself comfortable."

• • •

"Just keep on going," the woman commanded Ki. "I'll tell you what to do when the time comes."

Ki and his captor had been plodding along the stony floor of the high-walled canyon for only a short time. After she'd instructed him to take hold of the bar strap on her horse's bridle and lead the animal, Ki had begun cudgeling his brain for a way to break free. Each time he glanced over his shoulder, he'd seen the muzzle of her rifle trained on him.

Though a dozen ideas had flashed into his mind, none of them had seemed practical. The thought that he was the only person who could even guess at Jessie's whereabouts kept him from making any unplanned moves. He'd obeyed the unspoken command of the rifle digging into his spine rather than his urgency to break free.

Rain was still falling from the leaden sky, though it was now bursting in short fierce showers. Ki had begun trying to form a plan for freedom from the moment his captor had gotten behind him with her rifle ready, but he'd discarded each half-formed scheme as useless. The ground underfoot was too treacherous to ensure that the sudden moves he'd need to make in order to break free would be successful, and Ki knew quite well that any move he might make must be swift and certain.

He'd lost track of the number of plans he'd formed and discarded when the woman called, "We'll be coming to a break in the canyon wall in a minute or so. You'll see it first, but I know right where it is, so don't try anything."

"Are you saying I should turn in at the break?"

"That's right. It won't be long now till we'll be indoors where it's warm and dry."

She'd hardly finished speaking when Ki saw the

break himself. On his right a gaping space broke the high canyon wall. He reached it, and when he glanced through the wide *V* his jaw dropped and his eyes widened. Through the gap he saw the jagged line of a deteriorating stone wall and beyond it the blurred outlines of a half-dozen crumbling adobe buildings.

"That's where we're heading," the woman called. "Turn in. We'll be out of this damn rain in about two more minutes."

★

# Chapter 9

"What is this place?" Ki asked as they passed through the gap in the canyon wall and he saw the rain-obscured outlines of several buildings ahead. He stopped to get a better look at the structures.

"It don't look much like one now, but it used to be a Mexican army fort," the woman replied. "From what I've heard, they built it when Texas belonged to them—or when they thought it did."

"And the soldiers just walked away and left it?"

"Far as I know, they did. When old Sam Houston whupped 'em so bad they went on back to the other side of the Rio Grande and just left this place to go to rack and ruin. There's a few houses left, they're not much, but a body can still shelter in a few, like the one I'm living in now. It's pretty solid and the roof don't leak."

"Even in a rain like this one?" Ki gestured at the clouds. They still hung low, leaden and heavy, and were still releasing bursts of big spattering drops.

"This ain't a bad rain, alongside the winter ones.

Just the same, I'll sure be ready to get inside my house as soon as we get to it."

Even through the rain and at the distance that still separated them from the clutter of low-roofed adobe buildings, it was obvious that the little structures had received no attention for many, many years. Everywhere Ki looked he saw the signs of age and deterioration.

On some of the small houses the bricks had toppled from the upper corners, leaving long open V's that reached halfway to the ground. Cracks between the brick courses zigzagged halfway down the walls of most of the structures, and on many of the little hovels the adobe bricks curved inward or outward and gave hints that they were about ready to collapse.

Splintered planks that had once been doors hung askew from a single hinge on several of the houses; on others the doors were merely dark rectangles in the walls. A few of the windows had shards of glass remaining in them, and on a smaller number the splintered remnants of wooden shutters dangled by leather hinges. The crumbling little spread of disintegrating houses resembled a village shattered by an earthquake and abandoned by those who'd once lived there.

"How do you happen to be living in one of these places?" Ki asked.

"That's neither here nor there," she replied a bit tartly. When Ki did not comment, she pointed to one of the ruined dwellings. Before Ki could identify the one she was indicating, she went on, "We're headed for that one yonder. You can put your horse in where mine is."

"It's strange I've never even heard about this place," Ki said with a frown as they moved forward again. "As close as it is to the Circle Star."

"Is that where you come from?" she asked. When Ki nodded, she went on, "Then I imagine you'd be one of Miss Starbuck's cowhands?"

Ki had decided at the moment he'd been captured that the less information he provided, the stronger his position would be. He replied, "Of course. Why?"

"Oh, I've heard about the Circle Star Ranch. I guess most everybody has. And I suppose you've got a name?"

"Certainly. My name is Ki."

"Ki what?"

"My full name in Japanese is too hard for most people to say, so everyone just calls me Ki."

"I see. I guess I'll just do the same, then." She hesitated for a moment before going on, "Mine's Helena. Some folks call me Lena, but I don't like it when they do. Now let's save the rest for later and get inside without wasting our time talking."

Ki had been watching his captor while they were making their way from the road to the houses. He'd hoped that while they were talking, she'd lower the muzzle of her rifle or swing it away from its present threatening angle long enough to give him a chance to wrest it away from her, but the opportunity he'd wished for had not presented itself.

While they talked they'd reached the tumbledown adobe hut which Helena had indicated would be suitable for a temporary stable. Ki led his horse inside. A roan mare hitched to a splintered board lying on the packed-earth floor greeted his entrance by stamping its hooves and whinneying. Ki knotted the reins of his horse around the board to which the roan was tethered and stepped back along the animal's side.

He was reaching for the chincha strap that circled its belly when Helena stopped him.

"Leave your nag saddled," she said. "You can tend to it later on. Right now I want to go inside where I can get warm, and I'd guess you do, too. Just step past me and go on out the door. I'll be right in back of you with this rifle, and you've already found out.that I don't mind using it."

"Don't worry," Ki assured her. "Anything's better than being in this rain."

He went through the door opening without bothering to look behind him. He was sure that if he did look he'd see Helena with her rifle leveled at his back.

"You know which way to head," she went on, pointing to emphasize her words. "It's that house over there." Ki turned his head and saw her pointing to one of the adobe huts a dozen yards distant. "You walk in front of me. Don't try no tricks, if you know what's good for you."

Nodding, Ki started toward the building Helena had indicated. He had no doubt that his strange captor would use her rifle. He glanced over his shoulder only once. His quick look showed him that she was not crowding him. The muzzle of the rifle was trained on his back, and the distance was too great to allow him to whirl and reach the gun before she could trigger off a shot. Ki had no illusions; he knew that even his speed could not match that of a bullet.

"Open the door and go in," Helena ordered when they were only a step or two from the little building. "It ain't locked. First place, I ain't got anything worth stealing, and the second place, there's not anybody around to steal stuff."

Ki pushed the battered door open and stepped

inside. This cabin had a plank floor, which had seen a great deal of wear. Its boards were worn and splintered, but were still reasonably solid. The room held only a scarred and scratched pine table and a pair of straight chairs. Two cups and a couple of tin plates were on the table.

Equally well-worn shutters closed the windows that broke the thick wall on each side of the door. In one corner a small domed adobe fireplace held a heap of cold ashes. A skillet stood beside the low fieldstone hearth. At one side of the fireplace there was a pair of saddlebags standing near a heap of bedding. The shakedown bed looked scanty, a pair of blankets and a saddle pad folded to make a pillow.

"Damn it!" Helena snapped. As Ki turned his head to look at her, she went on, "I plumb forgot I'd burned all the wood. Come on. We'll go gather enough to keep us warm till this rain lets up and the sun comes out again."

Outside once more, Helena lifted the muzzle of her rifle and pointed it to the first house beyond the one she used as a stable. "We'll go over to that one. There's a bunch of loose wood inside."

Nodding, Ki walked ahead of her to the house she'd indicated. It had no door, and the window openings contained no frames. When he stepped inside, he saw several loose boards on the floor, but none small enough to be used in the little adobe fireplace.

"I make myself mad sometimes!" Helena exclaimed. "I'd plumb forgot I'd used all the little busted-up stuff! And these big thick planks sure won't fit in my fireplace. We'll have to go look in some of the other houses."

"I suppose these planks will do as well as any, if

108

they're broken up?" Ki asked over his shoulder as he indicated the thick boards.

"They'd do fine if a body could just bust 'em up. I don't carry an axe nor even a hatchet in my saddle gear."

"We won't need one," Ki assured her. He was already lifting the nearest of the heavy planks.

"Before you waste a lot of time, I tried my best to break up some of them boards," Helena said. "It can't be done. I even tried breaking 'em up with my rifle butt, but I stopped because I was afraid I'd bust my gunstock."

"Perhaps I will have better luck than you did," Ki told her.

He was stacking two of the long planks as he spoke, and now he stacked another pair parallel with those already in place. He'd left a gap a couple of feet wide between the boards, and now he placed a third plank across them at right angles.

Stepping back from the crossed board, Ki hunkered down for a brief moment, then leaped forward, thrusting down one foot in a *kakato* move as he dropped toward the single cross-plank. His sandal-clad foot hit the thick plank, and with the thud of its impact the crossed board splintered and broke.

"Well, I'll be damned!" Helena exclaimed. "How in hell did you do that, Ki?"

"In my country it is called *tamishiwari*," he replied. He was already arranging the board he'd broken across those which lay in parallel. He went on, "Now all that I have to do is to break off two more short sections, then I'll split them into pieces narrow enough to go into the fireplace."

"You expect to do that bare-handed, too?"

"Of course. The boards are already splintered and

cracked, and it's much easier to break them than it would be to split them with an axe."

"Go ahead and do it, then," Helena said with a nod. "Except I can't figure out how you can do what you just did, not without an axe or a hatchet."

Ki wasted no time in breaking two more lengths off the already-shortened board. Though he'd rather have had someone familiar with *tamishiwari* techniques hold the boards for him, he was sure that Helena would not have the strength to hold them firmly at the correct angle. He was also sure that she would not lay her rifle aside. Ki adjusted the unbroken boards in parallel, and across them he stacked the lengths he'd broken off with their centers above the gap.

Hunkering down at the end of the makeshift arrangement, Ki swung his arm once, then stiffened it and brought the entire outer edge of his forearm down on the center of the short stacked lengths of wood. The *tegatana* swing that he was using cracked all the splintered boards and broke them into widths no greater than a man's opened palm.

"I got to admit that's a real neat trick," Helena said as Ki started to pick up the short pieces of wood.

"It is not a trick," he told her. "It is only one of many exercises which are used in my homeland to teach students the art of what we call *karate*. In other lands it is called *aikijutsu* or *tae kwon do*."

"How long you figure it'd take if I was to ask you to show me how you managed to do that?"

"Three years, perhaps four," Ki said. "I am still learning after many more years than that."

"I reckon I'll have to pass, then," she said. "But you got warmed up by all that jumping around you done, and I'm still close to being froze to death. Let's go back over to my cabin and put a match to some of that firewood you've made."

Ki nodded. "It'll be good to get warm."

"Before we start, you might as well unsaddle," Helena went on. "Get your saddle pad and blanket. You can carry the wood back in your blanket. I guess you've already figured out that I don't intend to turn you loose right now, and you'll need your saddle gear for bedding, because I sure haven't got any."

"I hope you intend to give me a bite to eat?" Ki asked as he began to unbuckle the straps of the *cincha* that held his saddle in place. "I've worked up an appetite, breaking that firewood, and I didn't bring any saddle rations along with me."

"Oh, I won't let you go hungry," Helena promised. "Not that I've got too much grub, just some salt fatback and spuds. But you hadn't oughta complain. I'll be eating the same thing you are."

"You've probably noticed that I don't complain a lot," Ki told her. "And right now a slice of fried salt pork will taste as good as steak."

"I got to tie you up," Helena said to Ki. "Now that I've got warmed up and had a bite to eat, I'm getting sleepy. And I sure don't aim to take a chance that I'll doze off and give you a chance to jump me."

She and Ki were sitting on a blanket that she'd spread in front of the fireplace, where bright flames were now dancing from some of the pieces of wood Ki had broken. Helena's rifle rested across her thighs, where she'd kept it while cooking their scanty supper. Ki had already noted that its safety was off, for he'd been examining her closely while they ate in silence, making a meal of freshly fried bacon, soda crackers, and mild yellow rat-cheese.

111

It was the first good look he'd gotten of her. Helena had shed her slicker to reveal that she was wearing a cowhand's checkered flannel shirt whose globular bulges outlined her full breasts. Her thighs filled to stretching the Levi's denim jeans she had on, tucked into the tops of the calf-length high-heeled boots that cowhands called "ropers."

Her age could have been anywhere from thirty to fifty, though from the light lines on her brow and those which framed her thick heavy lips below her high prominent well-tanned cheekbones, Ki guessed that it was about midway between the two.

Helena's nose arched gently from thick dark eyebrows into swelling nostrils, her mouth was large, with heavy lips, and her chin curved into a sharp downward point. Her eyes were dark, and her light brown hair was pulled straight back from her forehead. It was cut raggedly to shoulder length, the trimming obviously a job she'd done herself.

"I was expecting you'd want to tie me up," Ki said. "And I won't fight you, I'd be a fool if I did, since you've got a gun and I haven't. But I'll sleep a lot better if you'll tell me why you took those shots at me and what you're doing here."

"Now, that's not any of your damn business," she replied, a note of sharpness creeping into her voice. "This is a free country. I go where I please and stay as long as I want to."

Ki realized at once that he'd made a mistake and was treading on exceedingly thin ice. Pitching his voice very carefully, he answered, "I didn't mean to trample on your toes. I guess I just let my curiosity get the better of me."

"Maybe you'd better not pry too much," Helena snapped. As though to emphasize her warning, she lifted the rifle off her lap and thunked its butt on the floor. Leaning forward, she went on, "It might be the excuse I'd need to get rid of you completely."

"I seldom make the same mistake twice," Ki assured her. "And I'm not going to try to get away as long as you've got that rifle in your hands. I never have seen anybody who could outrun a bullet."

"Now you're showing a little bit of sense," Helena said with a nod. "Not that you haven't before. Go on and spread your blanket and lay down while I get the rope."

"Rope?" Ki said, in a tone of voice that implied he was hearing the word for the first time.

"Of course. You didn't expect me to give you a chance to slip away. But don't worry. I'll fix the rope so that you won't be too cramped."

From the moment when Helena began trying Ki for the night, he saw at once that he was not the first person she'd bound up. When she ordered him to lie down on his face with his arms stretched along his sides, he obeyed without objection. There were few bonds from which he'd failed to escape during his life as a mercenary employed by warlords in the Far East.

Ki's opinion changed as Helena's work with the rope progressed, but by then it was too late, for the first moves she made in binding him virtually immobilized him.

Helena moved quickly, with the practiced speed of one who's done the same job many times. She knotted one end of the rope around Ki's left arm just above the elbow, then brought the line across his back, looped it around his right elbow, and secured it with a second knot. Taking a double turn of the rope around Ki's throat, she ran it down his body to knot his wrists together and finished her task by binding his ankles tightly.

"I never did see anybody get away from this kind of hogtie," Helena commented when she straightened up after finishing the knot that secured Ki's ankles. "And I guess I better tell you that I'm a real light sleeper. I'll have my rifle handy, and I'll be close enough to you so there won't be no chance of missing."

"I understand quite well," Ki replied. His voice did not betray his chagrin at allowing himself to be placed in his present situation, but he was sure that given enough time he could manage to free himself.

Though the time seemed to stretch interminably, only a few minutes passed after Helena blew out the lantern before nestling into her own bedroll when Ki heard her breathing settle into the rhythmic pattern of sleep. He waited another few minutes, testing the depth of her sleep by tapping the floor gently with his heels.

When Helena did not move and her deep breathing continued uninterruptedly, Ki began working to free himself. He tested the efficiency of his bonds by tugging his hands and arms with careful noiseless moves. With each small move Ki made, the loop around his neck grew taut, choking him. He could not fill his lungs with enough air to sustain him while he tried to pull into his bonds the slack that would allow him to bend forward and reach the knot at his ankles.

Absorbed in his efforts, Ki did not hear the soft almost noiseless rustle of Helena's blankets until he glimpsed her rising in her bedroll. He stopped moving at once, but she did not lie down again. Instead, she stood up and stepped up to Ki's side.

"You feeling uncomfortable? Or trying to get away?" she asked. There was no anger in her voice.

"Both, I suppose," Ki replied.

"You were doing pretty good," Helena went on. "If I hadn't been laying wakeful myself, I don't guess I'd've heard you."

"I'm not going to apologize for trying to get away," Ki told her. "I'm sure that if you were the one who's tied up, you'd've done the same thing."

"I don't suppose I can argue with you," Helena said. "But I know why I'm wakeful, it's because I've been without a man too long. And when I was tying you up, I noticed a lot more about you than your hands and legs." When Ki made no response, she went on, "After I saw that big bulge in your jeans, it was all I could do to keep my eyes off of it. And my hands, too. Ever since I got in my blankets I've been wondering about what you carry inside your britches-leg, and now I'm going to find out."

# Chapter 10

"You know this country better'n I do," Walters told Jessie. "How long you figure this damn storm's going to hold out?"

"That's anyone's guess," she answered. "Nobody can really predict the weather in this part of Texas. I'd just be making a wild stab if I tried to tell you. The rain could stop in the next few minutes, it could last for several hours, and it might even go on for two or three days."

"Well, I ain't in much of a mind to wait it out an awful lot longer. Now that we've got our part of this business settled, I want to get my money and move on."

"Please remember that it's my money you're talking about," Jessie said tartly. "And I'm as anxious to say good-bye to you as you are to get your hands on all that cash. If you—" She stopped short, aware that anything she added might make Walters suspicious.

He frowned. "If I what?"

Jessie shook her head. "Nothing important. I'm just tired and hungry. There are only two things I can think about right now. One is getting to where I can put on some dry clothes, and the other is sitting down to a good hot meal."

Walters gestured toward the cavern's opening as he said, "The way it's coming down now, I don't imagine you'd want to go outside, even if I'd let you. Not that you'd get far, unless you got a good-swimming horse."

Jessie's eyes had followed his motion. The big silver raindrops still splashed down, blowing into the entrance of their shelter. They were now pelting from the sky in such a volume that they obscured the view of everything beyond a narrow strip of the soaked earth extending a few feet from the cave's mouth.

"Looks like it's settling in to be a good one," he said. "And I bet that water running down this canyon's a foot or more deep by now. Even if the rain was to stop right this minute, it won't be safe trying to take a horse through that cut until after daylight."

"You seem to know a great deal about this place," Jessie said with a frown. "I suppose you've spent a long time scouting around the country here while you made your plans to kidnap me, working out all your moves?"

"Enough time for me to be sure about every move I've made so far," Walters said with a nod. "And this rain suits me just fine, because it's going to give your hands on the Circle Star a lot of extra work. If I know anything about ranches, the first thing they'll do is check up on the cattle, and that'll take a while on a spread big as yours. After they finish on the range is when they'll likely start worrying about where you've got off to. Chances are they'll go out

117

looking for you, but by then I'll have you tucked away safe and sound where they won't have a chance to find you."

"Where would that be?"

"That's something for me to know and you to find out," he replied. "But the place where we'll be heading when this rain stops ain't too far from here. That's all I'm going to say. Right now I'm going to unsaddle the horses and spread the saddle pads out and get some rest. Before I do that, I'll tie you up better'n you are now, and give you the pad off your horse so you can lay down and catch some shut-eye, too."

After Helena had announced her intention, Ki did not speak for a moment. Then he said, "I'm sure I know what you've got in mind, but you're not going to find out anything unless you take this choke-knot off my throat. My corpse wouldn't do you much good."

"I hadn't forgot," she told him. "I'll see you're getting plenty of air before I start in."

"I'm not even going to try to help you," he went on. "I like to choose my bed partners myself."

"So do I," she replied tartly as she began working on the knot of the choke-loop encircling Ki's throat. "But I guess you've found out that beggars can't be choosers."

Ki did not reply, nor did he allow his features to show any feeling as Helena pulled the rope from his neck. She did not disturb the remaining knots which secured his hands and feet. Ki kept his eyes on her face. Her expression had not changed, and did not change as she shifted her position enough to slide her hand under the bottom hem of his long loose pullover jacket.

118

Helena began exploring Ki's crotch with her hand. For a moment she was satisfied simply to stroke and squeeze him gently through the cloth of his trousers. As she prolonged her caresses and did not feel him swelling in response to them, a small frown started to nudge the smile off her face. Abandoning her efforts to arouse Ki by pressing him and stroking him through the hampering fabric of his trousers, Helena began feeling above Ki's crotch, seeking the fly-buttons of the garment.

A frown grew on her face when her groping fingers found neither fly nor buttons. As her hand reached the waistband of Ki's loose baggy pants without having encountered either, she started running her fingers along the waistband. Then she discovered the knot in his belt-cord. She tugged the knot free and yanked the trousers down from his hips, only to learn that she'd run into still another barrier, the ribbon-like crisscrossed length of linen strips that formed his *cache-sexe*.

"Damn it!" Helena exclaimed as she began tugging at the slippery fabric that was wound around Ki's waist and passed between his thighs to cover the vee of his crotch. "You chinks got the craziest ideas about what's fit for folks to wear! I guess you'll have to tell me how to go about getting this damn didy loose!"

Following the still-sketchy plan he'd hit upon, Ki did not reply. The thoughts that had started passing through his mind during Helena's insistent explorations were giving him ideas. He juggled a half-dozen variations of his scheme during the few minutes required for Helena to discover the tucked-under ends of the linen strip. By the time she'd found the end of the *cache-sexe* Ki still had failed to discover a real solution. He fell back on the Oriental custom of passive resistance.

During the few minutes of Ki's meditations, while Helena began to free him of the overlapping folds and creases of his *cache-sexe*, Ki managed to think of one solution to his problem. When at last she removed the band and tossed it aside, he'd formed his idea enough to begin putting it into practice.

When he felt Helena's warm hand closing around his flaccid shaft, Ki set his mind against allowing himself to respond to her caresses. She started exploring his crotch, fondling his limp cylinder, stroking and squeezing it gently. Ki maintained his firm control. No matter how much she handled him, he did not allow her caresses to affect him.

"Is there something wrong with you, Ki?" she asked when he still had not responded to her attentions after several minutes had passed.

Staring into the dimness of the cabin's roof, concentrating on his objective, Ki did not reply.

"Talk to me, damn it!" Helena demanded. She released him for a moment and rared back to sit on her heels, her eyes fixed on Ki's impassive face. He met her stare with his obsidian eyes, but still remained silent. Grasping his shoulders and shaking them, Helena went on, "Tell me what it's going to take to get you ready!"

Ki neither met her eyes nor spoke. When she'd waited for several moments without receiving a reply, she went on, "All right! If you don't intend to talk, I sure as hell won't keep on asking. But I know now what I need to do to get you inside me, and I've learned not to be a bit bashful about it!"

Bending forward above Ki again, Helena lifted his still flaccid shaft and started rubbing its tip over her cheeks. Ki immediately set his mind to ignore this new form of persuasive friction and successfully resisted the effects of her fresh caresses.

Ki found it was more difficult to keep himself from responding when Helena slid her lips over the tip of his still-flaccid shaft and he felt the soft rasping of her tongue. He concentrated on retaining his control and succeeded in preventing himself from responding to Helena's efforts with an erection. After she'd continued her oral caresses for several minutes and Ki still gave no signs of being aroused by her agile tongue's manipulations, he knew that he would win the silent battle.

Helena was nothing if not persistent. When she realized that her continuing efforts to rouse Ki were not going to be effective, she took him in even more deeply and began bobbing her head while continuing the movements of her caressing tongue. Minutes ticked away, each one seeming longer than the last, but Ki maintained his control.

Finally Helena pushed herself up and away from him. She did not leave him, but leaned back on her heels to look down into Ki's expressionless face. The puzzled frown on her face was visible even in the dim light cast by the waning fire.

"You got something wrong with you?" she asked.

Ki decided that the time had come to break his silence. He said, "Nothing that I know of."

"I've run into a few fellows that liked men instead of women," Helena went on. "Maybe you're one of them."

Ki shook his head. "No, I'm not. But I don't intend to be forced to do anything that I don't choose to do."

"Well, I'm sure glad I never did run into anybody

121

like you when I was in the life," she said. "But I've got sense enough to know when I'm beat. Here, I'll pull up your pants so you won't freeze later on tonight after the fire dies down. Then soon as I get that choke-knot tied around your neck again, I'm going to get myself some shut-eye."

"A very good idea," Ki agreed. "I'll enjoy sleeping myself."

"Sure. I'd imagine you're as tired as I am, but I don't figure that'll stop you from trying to get loose." While they'd been talking, Helena had been restoring Ki's bonds to their original position. She went on, "Now, that'll do it. You just remember that I wake up easy and I'll have my rifle right where I can pick it up fast."

When Ki made no reply, Helena stepped back to her bedroll and stretched out. Ki refused to surrender so readily to the urges in his body that were summoning him to slumber. He watched Helena covertly until he was positive that she'd dropped off to sleep, then began once more to test his bonds and try to free himself. Though he could move more freely now that the choke-rope no longer limited his movements, all his efforts failed.

He looked at the dying fire. Only a few dark red fading coals remained, but Helena lay stretched on her bedroll between him and the fireplace. Her eyes were closed, and even in sleep her face still bore traces of the unsatisfied frown that had formed after her failure to arouse Ki. However, he saw no movement except the slow rising and falling of her blankets in the gentle regularity that accompanied deep sleep.

Ki began moving cautiously, worming along the uneven floor. He was forced to move with utmost caution, for at all times he had to be sure he was giving the choke-loop around his neck enough slack to allow him to breathe freely. The most direct path to the embers of the dying coals would have taken him across Helena's body. With her bedroll between him and the hearth, Ki had to crawl in a half-circle around her feet. As slow as his progress was, he did not make the mistake of trying to move faster. He knew that until he managed to free himself, silence was more important than speed.

Several times he was forced to stop while he allowed the throbbing pains in his wrists and ankles to fade. The floor's warped boards were badly splintered in spots and Ki knew how important it was to keep his hands free of injury from any of the long stabbing splinters that stuck up from the little hut's scarred and battered floor.

Though his advance toward his objective took much more time than he'd expected, Ki at last reached the stones of the hearth. He stopped then to give his hands a chance to recover from the strain he'd put on them. While he rested, Ki used the minutes to study the dying coals at close range and to plan the next moves he knew he must make.

Only a few red coals glowed in the little domed fireplace now. Most of them were at the rear, obviously beyond his reach. He looked around the shallow hearth, but saw nothing that would be of any help to him. Then he began studying the fireplace itself. The top of its arched opening was less than a yard above the bottom layer of hearth stones at the point of its greatest rise, and its greatest width, where its bricks rested on the hearth, was almost too narrow to accommodate his shoulders.

After he'd spent several minutes studying the opening, Ki saw plainly what he must do. Leaning back, he swiveled on his buttocks by pressing his heels on the hearth and twisting his torso around. He was facing the fireplace now. Bending his knees and raising them toward his shoulders, Ki planted his feet on the hearth and flexed the muscles of his thighs and calves to pull himself forward a few inches. The gain he made was small, but it was enough. He could now reach the brightest of the glowing coals with his feet.

Stretching his legs to the utmost, Ki lowered his heels to the bottom of the fireplace just beyond the large glowing coal he'd chosen. A quick forward twitch of his legs started the red coal rolling toward him, and a second twitch placed it within reach. Ki lowered his bound feet until the strands of rope around his ankles touched the glowing surface of the coal.

Almost at once a thin coil of smoke began curling from the strands of rope, and after several seconds passed Ki began to feel a trickle of warmth radiating from the glowing coal. Then the heat reached his bare ankles, and within a few moments the heat grew into a stabbing pain. Ki banished the thought of pain from his mind, and at the same time began to stretch his knees apart. The rope-coils were still unyielding.

While Ki had been making his effort, the smoke rising from the rope strands had become thicker. Ki noticed the change. He pulled his knees together, then suddenly thrust them apart, putting all the muscle-pressure he could muster into an attempt to break the smoldering rope. He was still within the limits of his endurance when the bonds of his ankles parted and his legs were suddenly freed.

Ki flexed his knees quickly to draw his feet away from the smoking ember and the smoldering coils of rope that had fallen beside it. He did not stop to rest after his successful effort, but extended one leg until his foot was beyond the still-glowing coal. He kicked back, and his heel struck the ember and drove it almost to the edge of the hearth.

Now the glowing coal was behind him. Swiveling on his buttocks, the move easier now that his legs were free and he had the use of his feet, Ki strained to see the exact location of the ember that he'd kicked from the rear of the fireplace. He glanced at the arch of the fireplace to orient himself and saw that in order to reach the glowing red lump, he'd be forced to bend perilously far backward. This did not delay his next move. Jackknifing from his waist, he flattened his feet on the hearth and pushed himself backward until the coal was so close that he could feel its heat on his hands.

Ki inhaled deeply to fill his lungs with air. Then he clenched his teeth and drew his muscles taut as he hunched his shoulders and began lowering himself to place the rope around his wrists in contact with the coal. His muscles protested and the loop around his throat grew taut as he began lowering his hands slowly. His only guide was the heat radiating from the smoldering ember, and he had to swivel on his buttocks with slow careful moves until the heat was greatest above his wrists.

Although the deep inhalation he'd taken moments earlier had filled Ki's lungs with air, he was already beginning to feel the need to breathe freely. He tightened his control on his chest muscles as he slowly straightened his back while he lowered his arms to allow his wrists to touch the glowing coal. In spite of the sudden onrush of pain, Ki held his position while an acrid wisp of smoke trailed across his shoulders as his bonds started to char.

Pain from his wrists began creeping up Ki's forearms, and his lungs felt as though they were about to burst, but he ignored both warning signs. Then, with a faint hissing whisper of sound, the rope snapped and his wrists were free. So was the noose around his neck, and for the first time in what had seemed to be an eternity, Ki allowed himself to relax.

Though his chest was burning, he could now breathe freely. He also felt the welcome sensation of the muscles in his biceps and the long cordlike strand of the trapezius muscle along his shoulders relaxing, though they still protested a bit each time he moved. Ki pulled his arms together in front of him and began flexing them and humping his shoulders to ease the effects of the strain and restore the usefulness to his muscles.

He glanced at his wrists, and even in the feeble glow of the fast-fading fire he could see the bubbles of small blisters beginning to puff up on the backs of his hands. However, the pain of his burns was lessening now that his arms were away from the coals and exposed to the cooling air that had started trickling into the hut. Ki transferred his attention to his fingers. He spread them, arching them several times in the dragon claw, then formed a fist. To his relief, he discovered that he could move them without any loss of control or flexibility.

Now Ki was free to give his full attention to Helena. His moves had been virtually noiseless, and she'd slept soundly though the entire time Ki had required to free himself. She was still in a deep slumber, and did not stir when he stepped carefully up to her pallet and lifted the rifle she'd placed so carefully on the floor beside her blankets. Walking back-ward now, his eyes fixed on the sleeping woman, Ki carried the rifle across the room and placed it on the floor.

Returning to the fireplace, Ki gathered up the lengths of rope that he'd left on the floor after lib-erating himself from his bonds. Returning to Hele-na's side, he leaned over her and shook her shoulder gently.

"What's the mat—" she began as her eyes popped open. She started to sit up, but Ki's hand was still on her shoulder and he pressed firmly to hold her back pinned to her bedding. Then she came fully awake and stared up at Ki, her eyes opening fully when she realized that she was looking up at him and that he was holding her to the floor with the firm but not hurtful pressure of his hand.

"How the hell did you get loose?" she asked.

"That's not important," Ki told her. "What is im-portant is that I'm not your prisoner any longer. Our positions have been reversed."

"I'd swear on a stack of Bibles that I tied you so you couldn't move a muscle without choking!" she said.

"And you were wrong," he replied calmly.

"Damn it! I always knew you chinks was—" Hel-ena blurted. She stopped short when Ki's reminder belatedly sank home.

"Sneaky and not to be trusted," Ki finished for her, but there was no anger in his voice.

"Now, I didn't say that!" she protested.

"Not aloud. But it was what you had in mind."

Helena ignored his words. She asked, "Well, now that you've got free, what do you figure to do?"

"That will depend on you," Ki replied. "I'm sure

that you know a great deal more about Harry Walters's plans than I do. Now you will have the opportunity to share them with me. After I've heard your story, I'll decide what to do. How pleasant or unpleasant that is will be entirely up to you."

★

# Chapter 11

Involuntarily, Helena glanced at Ki's hands as though seeking assurance that he had indeed escaped his bonds. When she saw their condition, reddened and blistered, her mouth dropped open and a frown formed on her face.

"What in hell happened to your hands?" she gasped. "Why, they're raw as fresh meat hung up in a butcher shop!"

"I burned away the rope you had me tied with," Ki replied calmly. "It was the only way I could get them free."

"Don't they hurt?"

"A little," he answered. "But I can stand more pain than I'm feeling now without complaining."

"Complaining or not, that's a nasty bunch of burns you got," she said with a frown. "They need tending to right now."

"I don't have time," Ki replied.

"You've got more time than you've got hands!" Helena retorted. "Now, there's a bucket of lard in that little pile of groceries and rags and stuff over in the corner. I'll make you a deal. You get the lard and rags, and I'll get them burns soothed and bandage 'em up for you, and I won't pull no tricks while I'm doing it."

Ki recognized the sincerity in Helena's voice. He thought for a moment. In spite of his efforts to ignore the pain he'd been feeling since he'd freed himself, his hands were smarting and burning, and he remembered the ring of truth in Helena's voice when she'd made her offer. He was also wise enough in the ways of those on the wrong side of the law to protect himself from their deceits.

"I can't risk untying your hands," he said. "If I did it'd just tempt you try and get away."

"I can't work with my hands tied! Don't you figure you're smart enough to keep me from getting away?"

Ki read surrender in her words and countered quickly, "Let's say instead that I think you're smart enough to buy your freedom."

"For how much?" Helena asked.

"I'm not interested in money. But in addition to your bandages, I want information."

"Such as what?"

"I want you to tell me why you're here and who you're waiting for. In return for the information you give me, I may even let you leave."

Helena was silent for a moment, then she said slowly, "I guess that's a fair trade. I'll fix your hands, and while I'm doing it I'll tell you what-all I know."

Making a quick decision, Ki nodded. "And I'll take you at your word. I'll get the things you need and untie you, and we can talk while you're taking care of my burns."

In the spot Helena had indicated, he found a towsack that held a pint bucket of lard among a little gaggle of air-tights and a sack of cornmeal and one of flour. There were a few stringy rags in the bucket as well. He carried the the bucket and rags back to Helena and freed her hands. She began sorting through the rags, putting aside those she wanted. When she had a small pile beside her, she opened the bucket and started rubbing the rags she'd chosen in the lard.

"Just squat down here by me," she instructed Ki. "I swear not to play no tricks. I can work and talk at the same time, but I don't imagine you're going to like what I'll tell you."

Ki's expression did not change as he followed Helena's instructions. Pitching his voice to indicate a total lack of surprise, he asked, "Why do you say that?"

"Because even if I promised, you won't be sure anything I tell you is true."

"I know enough about what's happened to separate the truth from a lie," Ki assured her. "You gave away the reason you're here the minute you stopped me out in the canyon."

"I don't know what you're talking about!" Helena protested.

"More lies aren't going to do you a bit of good," Ki said. "Especially not when I know you're lying. Just to clear the air between us, perhaps I'd better tell you what I know."

A frown of uncertainty had formed on Helena's face while Ki talked, and her voice did not carry its earlier assurance when she replied, "Go ahead. It'll be a lot easier on both of us if all I've got to do is fill in what you might've missed."

"Here's what I'm sure of," Ki began. He spoke

131

slowly and confidently, choosing his words carefully, thinking of the best course he could take to keep Jessie from harm. "You're waiting here for a crook who's going by the name of Harry Walters. He's been at the Circle Star Ranch posing as a Texas Ranger looking for cattle rustlers who don't exist. Pretending to be a ranger was Walters's way of getting Jessie Starbuck's confidence so he could kidnap her. From the evidence I've found, that's what he's done, and when I ran into you I was sure this is the place where he was heading."

"I don't guess I need to try helping you so far," Helena said. "You been right all along the line up to now."

"Walters hasn't gotten this far by now," Ki went on. "Or you wouldn't still be here waiting for him. Somewhere along the way he stopped to shelter from the storm. Right now he and Jessie are somewhere between here and the Circle Star. All I'll need to do is backtrack until I find them."

She frowned. "You don't think they might not've come down the canyon at all?"

"That's not possible," Ki replied. "I tracked then far enough to be sure before this storm hit. I'm sure that he and Jessie are still in the canyon. There's no place between here and the Circle Star where they could've turned off."

While Ki talked, a frown had grown on Helena's face. When she spoke, her voice lacked its former assurance. "All you've told me is a bunch of guesses!"

Ki ignored her protest. He went on, "Kidnapping's a hanging crime, but I'm sure you know that. I'd imagine you'd like to stay alive."

"Now, wait a minute!" Helena frowned. "I don't

aim to hurt anybody, let alone kill them! Why, if I'd've wanted to kill you—"

"That's one of the reasons I'm telling you all this," Ki broke in. "Because when you jumped me yesterday, you talked instead of shooting."

"Maybe if you'll tell me what you expect me to do—" she began.

"Not a great deal," Ki said quickly. "Walters won't be expecting anyone except you to be here. I'm only interested in getting Jessie Starbuck away from him."

"And you'll stand up for me, if I help you?"

Ki nodded. "That's what I'm trying to tell you."

"Go ahead and tell me what you want me to do, then."

"You don't need to do anything when Walters gets here," Ki went on. "I can handle him by myself. But if you want to stay out of prison after I turn both you and him over to the law, you'll be in the witness stand testifying against him when he comes to trial."

"I didn't start out to hurt anybody," Helena said. "And I still don't aim to, if I can help it."

"You could be hurting Jessie Starbuck if you don't tell me the truth, or if you hold back anything."

"If Harry's scheme's worked out so far, you don't need to be worrying about Miss Starbuck," Helena told him. "Because she's likely to be on the way here right now."

When Ki replied, his voice did not reflect the satisfaction he felt. Instead, it was almost casual.

"Yes, I know," he said. "But he didn't figure on a number of things that have happened that weren't included in his plans."

"Well, why in hell are you asking me a lot of

133

questions about Harry's plans, if you already know what they are?"

"I'm not answering questions," Ki said firmly. "I'm asking them. From what you've let drop without intending to, I'm sure that you'll be very helpful."

"You ought to be smart enough to get the idea that I can't tell you something I don't know."

"Surely you know when Walters was to get here with Miss Starbuck," Ki suggested. Then he decided to shoot for the moon and went on, "That's why you've been so nervous. He's overdue, isn't he?"

"It's just this rain that's slowed him down," Helena said. "I was here a while back when it wasn't raining near as hard as it is now, and the trail got just like a little river in no time at all. We had to stop and wait it out, and then it was so muddy that we couldn't make good time."

Ki was quick to catch Helena's slip of the tongue. He asked, "When you say 'we,' I suppose that means you were with Walters?"

"Now, I didn't say that!" she protested. "Harry said I wasn't to—" Helena covered her mouth with her hand when she realized she'd been guilty of a second indiscretion.

Breaking in quickly, Ki finished her reply. "You weren't supposed to talk about Walters or his plans with anybody."

"Yes, damn it! But how'd you get to know so much?"

"That's not important. You'd already told me what I needed to know. It was very easy to figure out the rest of it."

"Of course, there's a few things you haven't tumbled to, yet," Helena said.

Hardening his voice, Ki told her, "You'd better

start filling the gaps, then. I want to know the whole scheme that you and Walters have been trying to pull off."

"You've already guessed just about everything there was to it," she replied. "Harry was going to bring Miss Starbuck here, and I'd tend to her till he got the ransom money. Then we aimed to scoot down to Mexico and buy one of those big hacienda places and just enjoy living."

"You're sure he was going to bring her here for you to keep safe?" Ki insisted. "He wasn't planning to kill her after he collected the ransom, so she couldn't be a witness against the two of you if your plans didn't work out?"

"Oh, dear Jesus!" Helena exclaimed. "I didn't remember until you said what you just did! A night or two before Harry took off for the Circle Star, he'd been hitting the bottle a mite too much. Maybe I had, too, because I'm just remembering what he said. . . ."

Ki waited for her to go on, but Helena had covered her mouth with her hand and was staring fixedly ahead.

"What did he say?" Ki asked. "Tell me!"

"That he'd take care of things so we'd never have to worry about money or about going to jail again. And you know what that means as well as I do. He don't intend for you or Jessie Starbuck to get out of this alive!"

Lying awake on her makeshift bed, Jessie stared into the darkness beyond the dying light of the feebly flickering fire. She listened to the raindrops splashing into the stream of water that was now rushing down the canyon. It was easy for her to form a mental picture of the canyon because just before sunset, while Walters was attending to the new fire, she'd had the chance to get close enough to the cavern's entrance to study the terrain outside.

Even at that time evening shadows had already begun to darken the cave's interior, but the limited landscape beyond its mouth had still been plainly visible. Fat raindrops were spattering off the loose rocks that were just outside the high arch of the cave's mouth and dimpling the surface of the brown roiling water of the runoff stream beyond. On the opposite side the high steeply rising bluff that limited her vision was striated with narrow bubbling channels cut by the blinding downpour.

Jessie had noticed that the edge of the swirling current was within a scant dozen feet of the entrance, and since that time the rain had shown no signs of letting up. Darkness veiled the cave's mouth now, but occasionally a gust of wind heavier than usual brought a swirl of drops just inside the entrance where they glistened briefly in the scant light given off by the dying fire as they dropped to the ground.

Jessie's mind had been busy trying to form a plan of escape even before the onset of darkness would cover her movements. Almost an hour had passed since she'd been deprived of the freedom to leave her blanket bed and move around. The first warning had come when she saw Walters go to his horse and pull several leather saddle strings out of the cluster that dangled from one of the pommel rings.

She'd realized at once that Walters intended to tie her up before he went to sleep. The move was one that Jessie had anticipated, and her carefully neutral expression had not changed when he stopped beside her and gestured for her to get to her feet.

"I don't guess you're used to having anybody tell you what to do," he'd said as she stood up. "But you're not in charge here. I'm getting a mite sleepy, and I don't aim to let you slip away while I'm dozing."

"You really don't have to worry about me trying to escape," Jessie had replied. "From the sound of that water running down the canyon, only a fool would risk trying to wade in it. Why, it must be knee-deep out there by now."

"Likely it is," he'd said with a nod. "Maybe even deeper. If I was asked to go wading in it, I'd say no thanks. But there's times when even sensible folks take chances, and I figure this is one of 'em." He lifted the hand holding the saddle strings and dangled them in front of her as he commanded, "Now, hold out your hands for me."

Little as she liked the idea of obeying him, Jessie realized that she had no alternative. She'd raised her arms and extended her hands with the insides of her wrists pressed together, but Walters had shaken his head.

"You know better'n that," he'd chided her. You ought've figured I wouldn't fall for such an old worn-out trick. Now, cross your wrists flat, one on top of the other one, and don't try to twist and turn 'em around while I'm tying you.

Jessie had kept her face expressionless and did not try to move her wrists while he bound them. She'd had only a slim hope that he might be unaware of the ease with which wrists tied bottom-to-bottom could be freed from even a tight binding. She watched while Walters crossed and recrossed the leather thongs, weaving them in crisscross fashion over and under and between her hands and arms.

Finally he'd looped the strips in several tight wraps around both wrists and tied them off with double square knots in the narrow space between her pressed-together wrists.

"That's so you can't get at the knots to loosen 'em with them pretty teeth of yours," he'd said, grinning. "I reckon now we can both sleep, but maybe yours won't be as comfortable as mine."

"That wouldn't worry you, of course," Jessie told him. "But I'll manage to get all the rest I need. Now, if you'll just spread my saddle blanket as you promised, I'm ready to go to bed."

From the moment Jessie had stretched out on her saddle blanket, rest had not meant sleep. Her bound wrists were a vexing annoyance that kept her from moving freely, and Walters had drawn the saddle strings so tightly around her wrists that her hands soon grew numb. However, overriding everything was Jessie's firm resolve to escape from the cavern in spite of the rain which was still gusting outside.

For an hour or longer the quiet within the cave had been unbroken except for the rain sounds and the few internal intrusions on its stillness. These were provided by Walters, who occasionally loosed a nasal snort from his bedroll, or by one of the horses grating its hooves and snorting as it tested the tether which kept it confined to the small triangle at the back of the cave.

Outside, the continuing noise of raindrops splashing into the torrent flowing along the floor of the canyon and the rumbles of the rushing current were louder than the faint sounds originating inside the cave. These were constant sounds, and as her hours of imprisonment stretched out, Jessie was only subconsciously aware of them.

From the beginning of her captivity she'd watched Walters closely, trying to deduce what he intended to do after the rain stopped, but beyond guessing that he'd been planning his moves for weeks, perhaps months, she'd gotten nowhere.

By now Jessie was sure that Walters had help waiting somewhere ahead. She had also concluded that he'd been planning his crime for several months, though she had only three vague clues on which to base her deductions. One was his familiarity with the terrain. The other two were a bit more solid: the store of firewood to which he'd gone unhesitatingly, and a heap of aging horse manure at the back of the cavern.

Ideas for eluding Walters in the outside darkness had come thick and fast into her mind for the first few moments after she'd lain down. All the ideas ended in the discard when she projected them in her mind against the backdrop of the continuing rainstorm and the bonds which made her hands almost totally useless.

After the first few minutes of painful chafing Jessie's wrists had grown too numb to feel the pain of the biting saddle strings. So had her hands, and she realized clearly that their use was vitally necessary. If she did manage to escape successfully, she would require their unrestricted usefulness to survive in the darkness and the deluge.

*What I need*, she told herself silently, *is some kind of grease. Saddle oil, or soft-soap or butter. All I've got is rainwater, and there's certainly plenty of that.* Then the thought struck home. *Water might do the trick, at that. Wet leather stretches, even if it's been tanned. And there's certainly plenty of water right outside.*

Jessie was not one who looked kindly on delay, and her action followed her thought immediately. She sat up and, after an unsteady first effort, managed to lever herself to her feet. Though the darkness inside was almost total, the opening of the big cavern outlined in a lighter shade of gloom served as Jessie's guide. Walters had been careful to place his bedroll between her and the cave mouth, and to be sure that she did not stumble over him, she followed a circuitous route toward the brighter shade of black that marked the yawning mouth.

As she drew closer to the V-shaped opening, the splashes of rain grew louder, and to them was added the occasional whistle of the wind which carried the storm. When she was within a half-dozen feet from the cavern's mouth, an occasional light touch of spray reached Jessie's face. After she'd reached the opening and stopped just inside the high triangular opening, the fine spray brushed over her constantly.

While the heavy clouds masked both moon and stars, Jessie could tell that rain was still pelting down by the tiny whitish pocks its drops raised when they hit the surface of the run-off water. Although the downpour veiled the narrow strip of land between her and the gleaming black stretch of the water that was rushing along the canyon's bottom, it did not hide the humped lighter blobs which revealed the location of an underwater boulder, nor the small light-hued splashes which were caused by raindrops hitting the surface.

Jessie sensed rather than saw the slope of the opposite side of the canyon, for darkness and the rainfall were veiling them totally. All that she could really be sure of was that the rise across the streaming flooded valley floor was as precipitous as the high slope which contained the cave. It rose with only a suggestion of a slant and was broken by vaguely visible blotches where partly embedded boulders or the underlying limestone surfaced.

Returning her attention to her more immediate problems, Jessie examined the narrow strip of dark earth that stretched from the cave's mouth to the edge of the rushing water. Her vision had adjusted to the outside darkness now, and she saw no obstacles in her path, but she stepped cautiously while making her way to the water's edge. She stopped there, and maintaining her balance a bit precariously, hunkered down within reach of the roiling stream.

★

# Chapter 12

Icy cold enveloped Jessie's hands when she leaned forward and plunged them forearm-deep into the water's black surface. She'd held them submerged for only a few moments when the icy water began to have its effect. First Jessie became aware that her fingers were losing their ability to move and to feel. She wriggled them, but was unable to tell whether or not they were moving. With incredible speed the icy chill traveled past her wrists and began to move up her forearms. Her elbows were not in the water, but soon they also felt icy cold.

By the time the traveling numbness reached that stage, Jessie had begun to shiver, not constantly, but at shorter and shorter intervals. Then the chill started creeping up Jessie's upper arms toward her shoulders. The sense of feel was now completely gone from her hands. She tried to flex her fingers, but with no sensation to guide her she was unable to decide whether or not they were moving.

Jessie kept her hands and wrists submerged until

she could no longer endure the paralyzing numbness. She lifted her hands from the water and shook them vigorously. Cold droplets arced away from them. She waved her arms up and down in front of her and for several minutes, and when she flexed her muscles again she was sure that they responded more readily.

Her fingers began to tingle, and when she tested their mobility by closing one hand into a fist, she had no trouble in clenching it. Though she could not be sure, it seemed that her bonds were looser and her arms easier to spread than they had been when she'd tried to part them inside the cave. Warning herself mentally that she might be just indulging in wishful thinking, Jessie levered her elbows still farther from her ribs. Now she could feel the unmistakable stretching of the leather strings around her wrists.

Gritting her teeth to keep them from chattering, Jessie bent once more to lower her hands into the water. This time she let them remain in their icy wet bath for several minutes before removing them to test her bindings for slack again. There was no mistaking the stretch that she felt now when she moved her arms. The rawhide strings were less resistant; they no longer cut into her wrists when she bent her elbows. She stretched her arms in front of her, then bent her elbows while bringing her bound wrists as close as possible toward her chest for what she hoped was the last stretching.

Jessie's hope was realized. The saddle strings were much more elastic now. When she straightened her arms and tried to pull one hand through the slackened loops, it slid easily past the confining strips. No real effort was needed, and she felt no pain when she was freed from the sodden thongs. A quick flick of her arm enabled Jessie to shake the limp leather loops off the wrist to which they were still clinging, and suddenly she realized that both her hands were free.

Using them was another matter. Chilled muscles protested when Jessie closed her hands into fists, and she opened them quickly. She began rubbing her hands together to bring back their feeling, and after several moments their icy numbness began to diminish. Now she started flexing her fingers, spreading them, closing them into fists, feeling their usefulness return.

While she waited she began cudgeling her brain, trying to come up with a plan that would get her out of her present predicament with a whole skin.

Returning to the cave, Jessie stopped just inside its entrance. Only a handful of coals remained glowing in the small circle of the dying fire. They were slowly fading to a dull red, but in the almost-total blackness they shed enough of a dim light to enable her to orient herself. In the rear of the cavern the horses were vague forms visible chiefly because their still-wet coats took on a shimmering sheen that reflected the glow of the small heap of glowing embers.

Walters's blanketed form was a dimly outlined huddle between Jessie and the fading coals. His upturned face was barely visible; it appeared to be a lighter blurred oval surrounded by the gloom. Looking at him, Jessie wondered where he'd put her Colt and how she was going to get the revolver away from him.

She had no illusions about Walters's strength. Knowing that it was greater than hers, she realized that in a hand-to-hand struggle, the odds would be overwhelmingly against her. As she stood frowning thoughtfully, one of the horses tossed its head and whinnied. Involuntarily, Jessie glanced in its direction and glimpsed a glint of metal reflected from a buckle on the moving animal's headstall.

A bit impatiently, Jessie sought to regain the train of thought broken by the animal's noise and movement, but once more her effort was interrupted, this time by an idea bursting full-blown into her mind. She glanced once more at Walters, to make sure that his sleep had not been disturbed, then began moving with slow careful steps toward the horses.

Her feet rasping gently on the cavern's floor sounded loud in the total silence, and she'd taken only a few steps when one of her bootsoles came down on a loose stone. The grating of the leather against the rough surface underfoot was like the crackling warning given out by a ceiling that began to emit small popping noises in warning that it was on the verge of collapsing. Jessie stopped short and looked back at the pallet where Walters was sleeping, but saw no movement. She resumed her careful approach and reached the tethered horses.

Now the real job began. Jessie had no difficulty in picking out her own Circle Star mount, even in the darkness. She rubbed the animal's nose gently, and it tossed its head when it recognized her familiar hand. Slowly and gently Jessie began running her fingers along the horse's bridle strap. It was a task to which she was accustomed, though Jessie wished that the animal was Sun instead of a horse less accustomed to feeling her hands.

She would not allow anyone else to touch Sun, her magnificent palomino. Sun had been a pony when Jessie's father gave him to her, and Jessie had always insisted on being the only one to put on his bridle and saddle. Her apprehension vanished when the substitute mount she'd chosen stood quietly when she ran her hand along its jaw until she reached its bridle.

Jessie felt the polished nickle-plated bridle buckle and groped with her hand along it to the bit ring. The metal was cold to her touch, and she nodded with satisfaction as she fingered its smooth chill. Working by feel she removed the short length of leather strap attached to the buckle and freed it from the link strap.

As she turned and started back toward the mid-section of the cavern, she carefully rolled the short length of leather into a tight coil. It served as a handle for the buckle which she now held between her thumb and fingers.

Walters had not moved when Jessie reached his bedroll. He still lay on his back, breathing gustily. His face was a dim blur in the darkness, and when Jessie saw that she did not need to worry that he might awaken suddenly, she breathed a silent sigh of relief. She shifted the buckle and strap in her hand until she was sure of their alignment, then bent forward and lightly pressed one of the extended points of the rectangular buckle to Walters's throat, just above the pulse of his jugular vein.

When the fake ranger felt the cold metal tip of the buckle touch his neck, he stirred and grunted and started to lift himself from his bedroll. Even in the gloom Jessie could see his eyes pop open.

"Don't move an inch!" she commanded sternly. "This knife's got a needle point and I'll slide it into your gullet if you try to fight me!"

When Walters dropped his head back to the blankets Jessie followed his move with her hand, keeping the cold corner tip of the metal buckle pressed firmly against his skin.

"Where in hell did you get your hands on a knife?" Walters asked. His voice carried both surprise and anger.

In contrast, Jessie's voice was calmly level as she replied, "I'll leave you to wonder about that. And while you're wondering, just remember that it won't take much of a push on this knife to leave you very, very dead."

While she was speaking, Jessie was wondering how long her bluffing could deceive Walters. At the moment all that he could feel was the chill of metal against his vulnerable throat, but when the buckle's tip absorbed his body's heat and grew warm he'd be able to tell by its feel that it was not the needle point of a knife.

Jessie went on, "Don't move your hands suddenly. If you did that it might make me nervous."

"Don't worry," Walters assured her. "I'm not a fool."

"Now, I'm sure you've got your pistol where you can get to it in a hurry," she told him. "Get it out very slowly to where I can see it, then slide it across your blanket with your elbow until I can reach it."

Moving with a slowness that would have made a snail envious, Walters gingerly brushed the blankets aside with a boot toe and, when he'd uncovered his revolver, used the side of his leg to nudge the weapon along the blanket until it was within reach of Jessie's hand.

Jessie closed her hand around the weapon's rough butt and picked it up. As soon as her trigger finger slid through the trigger guard, her thumb levered the hammer back to full cock. She brought up the muzzle until it was level with Walters's eyes and only then let the strap buckle fall from her left hand to his blanket.

"Now dig out my Colt and hand it over," Jessie commanded. "I can use this gun of yours as easily as I can my own, but I'll feel more at home with mine, and I'd be very surprised if you don't have it within easy reach."

His every move showing his reluctance, but without raising his voice to complain, Walters lowered one arm to fumble beneath the tousled blanket until he'd found Jessie's Colt. He did not stand up or try to pick up the weapon, but nudged it with his elbow to the edge of the blanket.

Still holding the muzzle of Walters' pistol to his head, Jessie used the toe of her boot to snake her own Colt within easy reach. Without breaking the contact of Walters's weapon with his temple, she picked up her own revolver and with a few quick but cautious moves switched pistols and slid his Colt into the waistband of her skirt.

"That's better," she told him. "Now roll over on your face and stretch out, then put your hands behind your back."

Walters obeyed, but his moves were hesitant and reluctant. Jessie groped for the leather bridle strap that she'd dropped after taking Walters's gun from him. Slowly, because she kept her eyes fixed on Walters and worked only by feeling, she circled the strap around his wrists and pulled the end through the buckle.

A bare inch or so of the strap's tip protruded from the buckle, and Jessie had no intention of laying her pistol aside in order to use both hands to secure it. With only one hand available she had trouble pulling the tip far enough to secure it in the first buckle hole. Her persistence was finally rewarded, and when she was sure that Walters would not be able to free himself easily nor quickly, she breathed a relieved sigh and leaned back to sit on her heels.

"Now we can talk," she said.

"I got nothing to say," Walters told her. His voice was subdued, but sullen.

"You'd better change your mind," Jessie cautioned him. "I might give a little more favorable testimony in court if you tell me the whole story now, without forcing me to drag it out of you a word or two at a time."

"What do you figure I can tell you? Now, I know damn well you're a smart lady, Miss Starbuck. If you wasn't smart, you wouldn't know what to do to get free."

"I might return the compliment by saying you were smart to capture me, but failing to keep me your prisoner gives me a lot of doubt that you deserve any congratulations."

"Oh, you got a good reason to crow, all right," Walters told Jessie. "I bet it took you a lot of figuring to get loose. Now, I'm betting that you're bound to know what I was going to do, even if you had to guess a lot to figure it out."

"I wouldn't say that's exactly the case. For one thing, I don't yet know whether you've been working single-handed to kidnap me or whether you're part of of a gang."

"I don't see that makes much never-mind, now you've got yourself free."

"Of course it does. I want to know exactly what to expect before I decide what to do with you in the next few hours."

His voice defiant now, Walters snapped, "I'd just as soon let you stew about that."

"I'm sure you would," Jessie agreed. "But if you were supposed to meet somebody after you abducted me, and you don't show up, that somebody is going to come looking for you sooner or later. I need to know everything that you planned to do before I interrupted your plans, so that I can get busy and make some plans of my own."

"Suppose I just close up like a clam?"

"That's your decision, of course." Jessie's voice was still smoothly unruffled. "But I believe you'll change your mind after you've thought things out for a few minutes. Now, I'm getting a bit chilled on this cold hard floor. I'm going to tie your feet, and then I'll build up the fire. We'll finish our little talk later."

For the moment that followed Helena's revelation, Ki stared at her without changing his expression. Then a frown swept over his usually impassive face and he asked, "You're sure about what Walters told you?"

"Oh, I'm certain enough, all right. I just didn't tumble until just a minute ago to everything he was getting at. What you said sorta pulled everything together and stirred up my memory a little bit."

"And you didn't stop to think what he'd said about killing people could only mean that he was going to kill Jessie, so she wouldn't be on hand to give testimony against him in case something went wrong and you two were caught?" Ki asked.

"I guess I didn't think of it like that. But he never did come right out and say it."

Ki nodded. Then, pressing the advantage he saw

he'd gained, he went on, "When are you expecting him here?"

Helena shook her head. "He didn't set a time or day or anything like that. He just told me to keep watch along the canyon, and I'd see him when he got back."

"But he didn't tell you when to look for him?"

Again she shook her head. "Harry never was one to talk about what he intended to do."

"You've been with him on jobs like this before, I suppose?"

"I never was with him on one like this before," she replied slowly. "He's pulled a few jobs where I've stood lookout, like when he's stuck up a bank or a faro parlor, something like that. But I never knew of him of stealing a woman before now."

"Did you ever join a gang on a job with him?"

"I never did go with him on a job he pulled with a gang. There's been times when he's hooked up with one or another of 'em. I know from things he's let drop now and then that he done some cattle rustling with a couple of fellows called McNew and Coffelt. From what little I heard him say about 'em, they wasn't together very long."

"And Walters never was a Texas Ranger as he claimed to be, was he?" Ki asked.

Helena thought for a moment before replying, then she said slowly, "He might've been, way back sometime before him and me got hooked up together. But if he was, he never talked about it to me."

Ki could see clearly by now that if Helena knew anything worth his learning, he might be forced to spend more time worming it out of her than the information would be worth. Still, he could see no real alternative. Anything that would give him information about Walters would certainly be useful in planning his own moves.

"How well do you know the lay of the land up the canyon?" he asked.

"All I really know about it is this part right around here. Harry's done all the scouting between here and Miss Starbuck's ranch."

"You must know a little bit about it, from what Walters has told you. Now, he was on his way here with Jessie, and I think it's safe to figure that they must have stopped somewhere in the canyon when the storm hit. In the rain it'd have been easy for me to miss seeing where they left the trail."

"Sure," she said. "You'd have passed right on by them if they'd pulled off of it. Chances are you wouldn't even have known they were anywheres close."

"Well, do you know of a place between here and the ranch where they could've taken cover?"

Helena was frowning thoughtfully while Ki spoke. Now she shook her head and said, "I haven't been any farther up that trail than right here where we are now."

Ki had been so absorbed in listening to Helena and trying to relate her story to what had actually happened that he had not noticed the diminishing patter of raindrops on the roof.

"How far up the canyon have you been?" he asked.

"Not much more than a half-mile. There've been a couple of times when I'd ride a little ways with Harry when he'd go out to scout around."

"He went up to the Circle Star more than once, then?" Ki pressed.

"Oh, sure. Three or four times would be more like it."

"Studying the layout of the range, I suppose?"

"Sure. He said he needed to know every little bit about how the land lay and find out what was going on at Miss Starbuck's ranch before he worked up all his plans to grab her and bring her here."

"And he never did tell you what he planned to do after he'd captured here?"

"Well, now, there wasn't much need for him to do a lot of talking, and even if there had've been, Harry's not much on letting anybody know what he's thinking about when he goes on some sort of a job."

"And all along you've had a pretty good idea of the sort of scheme he had in mind?" Ki pressed.

Helena was silent for a moment, then she admitted, "I guess I did, only I didn't like to think much about it, knowing Harry the way I have for such a long time."

"How long would that be?"

"Going on three years."

"Then you ought to know him pretty well," Ki suggested.

"I guess I do. There's been good times and bad ones between us. But a woman can't be too choosy when she's getting along and don't see much ahead of her."

Ki nodded, then said, "You'd have to know Walters pretty well, then. From what you've told me, you must be pretty sure that he intends to hold her for ransom."

"Oh, sure. I already told you, he's said he's going to get a lot of money. But what bothers me is that a few times he's been drunk and started bragging about how smart he is. All he can talk about when he's like that is how he never has been fool enough to leave anybody alive that could stand up and testify against him in court if he got caught and had to be tried."

For a moment Ki said nothing, and when he spoke his voice carried a harshness which it seldom held.

"Come on," he told Helena. "We've wasted enough time. From what you've said, Walters is holding Jessie up the canyon somewhere between here and the Circle Star, and we're not going to stop until we find them!"

★

# Chapter 13

Jessie sat up on the saddle pads that had been her bed. She blinked once or twice, but the darkness did not diminish. She felt refreshed by the sleep she'd had after binding Walters's ankles and rekindling the dying fire, but wondered what had wakened her so early. She thought of Walters, and glanced at his motionless form. He was still sleeping, or feigning sleep, huddled on the blanket deeper in the cavern. Looking at him now reminded her of the reason she'd slept on a makeshift bed that gave off the odor of horse sweat.

Jessie had already finished binding the outlaw's feet the night before when she'd realized that she had no bedroll. After a moment's thought, she had decided not to take the chance that Walters might try to escape if she untied him and allowed him to stand up while she took part of his scanty bedding. Instead, she'd made herself a shortened bed of their horses' saddle pads and had slept well enough to feel rested now.

Turning to look toward the mouth of the cavern, Jessie saw it outlined faintly in the beginning dawn. Through the opening's wide-based triangle of dark ghostly gray, all that she could see was a thin strip of leaden sky above the distance-blurred rim of a small triangular section of the canyon's opposite wall. Rising to her feet, Jessie went to the cavern's opening and stepped outside.

Full daylight had not arrived and as yet there was not even a strip of rosy sunrise hue along the eastern horizon. The sky in that direction did show a thin line of daylight gray, and overhead the main canopy was shading from the deep blue-black of the western horizon to the graying hue that was slowly growing brighter in the east. The fading stars were dim and the floor of the canyon was still almost as dark as it had been during the night. Even so, enough brightness had been brought by the arriving dawn to allow Jessie to see some of the effects of yesterday's downpour.

Directly across from the canyon's mouth the steep side of the wide cleft's earthen wall was streaked with small dark gullies cut by the heavy rain. A few of them showed glints of water trickling along their bottoms, fed from puddles along the rim which were continuing to pour water down from the crest.

Big rocks that had been bared by rainwater cascading down the canyon's sides bulged from the steeply slanting wall. Some of the rocks were the size of a horse's rump, but most of them were no larger than a baby's head. The few exceptionally large puddles that had formed in the bottom of the canyon shimmered vaguely in the semi-darkness that had not yet been banished by the approaching daylight.

A few of these big pools remaining from the runoff

stretched from one side of the canyon to the other, and as she glanced at them Jessie realized that until they drained or were dried by the sun's rays the canyon floor would for all practical purposes be impassable. No sensible person would risk laming or perhaps even drowning a horse by trying to force it along the invisible sections of the bottom. She was beginning to wonder how long she would be forced to stay in the cave with Walters when the outlaw's voice broke into her thoughts.

"What's it look like outside there?" he called.

"Wet and muddy," Jessie replied. "We won't be able to move out of this place for quite a while."

"How long do you figure quite a while will be?"

"A day or two, at least. It's impossible to guess how long. You might know better than I do. I'd imagine you're better acquainted with this place than I am."

"That's likely so, but I never have been here when it rained like it did yesterday."

Jessie started to remind Walters that she was sure Ki and perhaps some of the Circle Star hands as well were going to be riding out looking for her soon, but decided quickly that she'd be making a mistake if she included that topic in any of their conversation.

"We're going to be mighty hungry if you've got plans to stay holed up here very long," Walters went on when Jessie did not reply to him. "I didn't figure on us having to stop anyplace on the way back down the canyon from your ranch, so I didn't ask your cook for some tide-over grub to put in my saddlebags. It didn't occur to me that we'd need any."

"And I don't even have any saddlebags," Jessie reminded him. "But I'm sure the ground will be firm enough in two or three days to give the horses the footing they'll need."

"Two or three days is a damned long time when your belly's empty," Walters said. "And if push comes to shove, it ain't all that far back to your ranch."

"I imagine we'll be able to survive." Jessie's voice was tartly unsympathetic. "Though I'm sure neither one of us will enjoy waiting."

"I hope you ain't got it in mind to keep me hogtied all the time," Walters went on. "Because right now I'm about as uncomfortable as a man can be when he wakes up of a morning, if you get what I'm driving at."

"I understand quite well," Jessie replied. "And if you'll be patient for a minute or two I'll untie you and let you step back to where the horses are tethered. I'll warn you now about trying to get away, because I'll be holding my gun on you even if it might embarass you."

"I take your meaning," Walters replied. "I ain't all that bashful, and even if I was, having you watch me's better'n letting my guts bust open."

"We understand each other, then," Jessie said with a nod. "The light's getting better all the time, and after I've tied you up again, I'm going outside and see if I can figure out a way for us to get out of here and go back to the Circle Star."

"If we keep having to pick our way through this mud so carefully, we're never going to get anywhere," Ki said.

"It's slow going, all right," Helena agreed.

For what seemed to have been an interminable period of time Ki and Helena had been working their way up the canyon. During the first half-mile the going had been relatively easy. For most of the distance they'd covered from their starting point, the walls of the big cleft had been far apart and they could weave in and out along its bottom, zigzagging to avoid the worst expanses of soft muddy unstable terrain that now dotted the central sections of its bed.

However, as they'd progressed, the gap between the high bluffs had begun to narrow. The ground was no longer relatively smooth, but studded with outcrops of limestone shale, and the current that had swept its surface during the storm had bared these areas and made them slippery. The night's storm had also left huge puddles of water along the canyon's bottom.

Some of the puddles spanned almost the entire width of the canyon floor. They'd tried to wade their horses through the first of these miniature ponds they encountered, but the effort to coax their mounts over the slippery treacherously yielding footing had brought them close to disaster a few times when the horses floundered and their hooves began sliding on the slick mud.

After two or three near-falls, Ki had decided that the only safe way to proceed was to hug the base of the sides and to cross from wall to wall only when absolutely necessary. He told Helena, "We won't try that again. Even if it means going a little slower, we'll skirt those big pools the rest of the way."

"You sure it's smart for us to keep pushing on?" Helena asked him after they'd spent a half-hour zigzagging back and forth, stopping often to look for a reasonably safe path ahead. "We're not making good time at all, and we ain't even sure we're heading in the right direction."

"You may not be sure, but I am," Ki replied. "That rainstorm yesterday evening came in from the west. I got caught when it reached me, and since I knew it would wash out any tracks that might have been left by Jessie and Walters, I started moving faster. I couldn't keep ahead of it, of course, the storm moved faster than I did. I'm sure that when it overtook Walters and Jessie, he knew about some sheltered place where he could take her to wait for it to pass, and I just went on by them in the storm."

"I guess that'd make sense," Helena agreed. "So by now they'd be started out this way again. It's likely we'll run into 'em not too far ahead."

"That's what I'm counting on," Ki said, nodding. "And I'm also depending on you to stay out of any sort of fracas that Walters might start."

"There ain't much way I could help Harry, even if he was to start something. And I know when I'm whipped, even if he don't. I figure that if I stay out of things from now on, it'll go easier for me later on."

"Just keep telling yourself that, and you and I will get along fine," Ki said. "The best thing you can do to keep out of trouble later on is to help me now."

"Now, I didn't promise that," she reminded him quickly. "I said I'd stay out of the way if you and Harry start butting heads."

"That's about as much as I'd expect," Ki agreed. "Just keep that in mind, and you and I won't have any more trouble."

They rode on in silence through the steadily brightening dawnlight. Everywhere they looked, the storm had left its marks. By this time they'd gotten accustomed to seeing the deep gullies cut in the canyon walls by the downpour, and had learned which

160

stretches on the floor of the deep gulch promised a safe footing and which sections to avoid.

Their course continued to be one chosen on the spur of the moment. From time to time they were forced to rein one or both of the horses aside to avoid an expanse of the too-yielding sand that was almost certain to hide an underlying stretch of the deceptively yielding clay. The rain-sodden clay seemed to suck a horse's hoof down suddenly and cause the animal to lurch and flounder wildly.

There was no such warning given the rider when a horse's hoof started to slip on a buried boulder. The only resource on which the horseman could rely was a well-learned skill. Avoiding a fall meant keeping a good grip on the saddle horn while the horse veered and swayed and reared and stamped on the soft mushy soil with its hind feet while rearing up and swiveling sharply to find a spot where it could safely bring down its forefeet.

Although their progress up the canyon was slow, Ki and Helena moved steadily ahead. The dawnlight soon gave way to the rosy hues of sunrise, and even more rapidly to the sunlit sky of full day. Now the full effect of the storm-brought rain could be seen clearly.

Huge patches of freshly exposed earth on the walls of the canyon showed where the rain-loosened soil had slipped away and created expanses of soft yielding soil on the canyon floor. Ki learned very quickly to avoid these as much as possible, skirting them when there was room to maneuver around them and guiding the horses along their edges when it was necessary to cross the lumpy, freshly dropped and yielding soil near their centers.

Still, the need to advance so carefully slowed their

161

progress, as did the softness of the footing. The horses could not maintain a steady gait, and the mud clods that formed on their hooves tired them unduly.

For the first few miles, where the floor of the canyon had been wider, when the clods grew too heavy for the already struggling horses, it had been possible for Ki to rein in on a stretch of solid ground and dismount long enough to scrape their hooves clean. The farther they advanced through the narrowing canyon, the soil became softer, the puddles on the floor bigger, and their progress slower.

Here the runoff had not really begun. The bigger puddles drained slowly, and there were times when they were forced to wade the horses through pools of still-standing water. Since neither the horses nor their riders could see solid ground, their advance across the areas where the pools remained became a careful plodding crawl rather than a steady walk.

"You think we'll really find Harry and the Starbuck woman up ahead?" Helena asked Ki when he straightened up and began swinging his hands to clear them of mud after a hoof-scraping stop.

"We'll find them," Ki replied confidently. "I don't think it's likely that they'd turn back and head for the Circle Star."

"You never know what that Harry's going to do," Helena commented. "Maybe that's why I've stuck with him such a long time."

"Don't let your feeling for him drive you to doing anything foolish when we catch up with him," Ki cautioned her. He swung into his saddle, toed his horse into motion, and they started again up the canyon, the horses picking their way carefully on the uncertain footing.

\* \* \*

"I ain't moved for such a long time that I'm beginning to feel like I'm already dead and buried in this place," Walters complained, breaking a long silence that had settled down within the cave. "I don't even feel like I've got feet anymore."

"You certainly can't be expecting me to sympathize with you," Jessie replied tartly. "I don't have any more sympathy for you right now than you had for me a few hours ago."

"That's not exactly what I was getting at. What I'm asking is how about you loosening up this hogtie you put on my legs and letting me walk around a few minutes, just so's I can get some feeling back into 'em?"

Jessie considered Walters's suggestion for a moment. Though she had no sympathy for him, she remembered the occasions when she'd been a prisoner of the vicious European cartel that she and Ki had battled for such a long span of years after the cartel's hired crew of killers had murdered her father. There had been times during those periods of captivity when she'd felt like making the same request that Walters was making now.

She decided that as long as she took the precaution of preventing him from running away or from launching a surprise attack on her, there was no reason to refuse him.

"Very well," she said. "But I'll have to hobble your legs. I don't intend to give you a chance to jump me or to start running. I won't free your hands, but I'll put a short hobble on your legs and let you walk around for a few minutes."

Stepping over to the horses without removing her eyes from Walters, keeping him under the threat of her Colt as she worked, Jessie began unbuckling one of the rein leathers from the animal's headstall.

"Come over here close to what's left of the fire where I can see what I'm doing," she told him. "You'll have to lie down while I fix your feet."

"Lay down? Fix my feet? Just what're you figuring to do, if you don't mind me asking?"

"I told you. I'm simply going to put a hobble on you. You can take short steps, but you won't be able to run."

Walters hesitated for a moment, then he nodded and said, "I guess what they say about beggars not being choosers is right. Go ahead and fix me up whatever way you've got a mind to."

Walters was lowering himself to the cavern floor as he spoke. Jessie returned carrying the long strip of leather. She stopped beside Walters and bent to free his ankles from the old binding that had held them, wrapped an end of the rein strap around his left leg just above the old short hobble, and looped the other end around his right leg. She removed the old short hobble and tested the improvised bond to be sure it could not be kicked free easily.

Rising to her feet Jessie drew her Colt and nodded as she said, "All right. I'm sure you can stand up by yourself. Now, stay away from the mouth of the cave while you're taking your exercise. I don't need to tell you that I'll shoot you if you try to get away."

"Well, I guess I've got to give you credit," Walters said grudgingly as he managed to lever himself to a standing position. He glanced down at his ankles and shook his head as he went on, "You sure don't miss any bets when you set out to do something."

"I try not to," Jessie replied, taking a step away from him. She rested her hand on the butt of her holstered Colt as she spoke. "Now, don't do anything foolish just because I've let you have a little bit of freedom. I'll cut you down without a bit of regret if you try to get away."

"I don't doubt that for a minute," he told her, taking an experimental step.

Walters wobbled a bit unsteadily when he misjudged the length of the strap that limited his stride, then recovered his balance and took another step. This time his judgment was better and he did not stretch his foot forward far enough to disturb his equilibrium.

"Remember, if you try to get too close to me, or try to make a run for the outside, I won't waste my breath warning you," Jessie said as she watched Walters making his experimental moves. "I'll just shoot. I haven't any compunction whatever about shooting an outlaw like you've turned out to be, even if you aren't holding a gun in your hand."

"Now, you don't have to worry about that," Walters assured her. "If I've got any sense at all, I've got enough to know when I'm bucking a stacked deck. And that's sure what you're dealing from."

"None of this was my idea," Jessie pointed out. "Now, go on and do your leg stretching. I don't intend to leave you on a loose tether very long."

"What I've got to do first is go back by where the horses are and answer nature's call," Walters said. "I don't know what it is that works on a man when he's tied up this way."

As the outlaw spoke he was turning to head for the rear of the cave. Jessie watched him as he stepped behind one of the horses. In the gloom that veiled the rear of the cavern she could not tell which of the animals now stood between her and Walters, but she did not like the idea of letting him out of her line of vision even for a few minutes.

"Hurry up and get back out in the open where I can see you!" she called. "Remember, I—"

Jessie stopped short and dropped flat when Walters's head popped up above the back of one of the tethered horses, and she glimpsed the glint of blue steel in his upraised hand. Jessie was drawing her Colt when the shot Walters triggered off reverberated through the cave. The slug whistled over her head and screeched as it ricocheted off the high stone wall behind her.

Before the resonance of Walters's shot died away, Jessie had her Colt in her hand and was trying to locate him in the gloom that shadowed the back wall of the cavern. All that she could see was the shadowy bulky forms of the horses.

"You might as well come out and give up!" Jessie called. "I'm between you and the cave mouth, and you'll never make it to the outside if you try to get away!"

"I'll take my chances!" Walters called back. "You know, you ain't as smart as I've heard, Miss Starbuck. Seems to me you played the fool when you didn't stop to think I might be carrying a backup gun in my saddlebags!"

Jessie had already realized how Walters had tricked her, and she was now regretting her own failure to think that he might have a backup gun.

At the same time she told herself that her warning to the outlaw was true: there was nothing that Walters could use for cover between his present position in the back of the cave and its mouth. In order to get out he'd be forced to cross a barren space of sixty or seventy yards, and she had no doubt of her ability to get in a telling shot before he'd taken a half-dozen steps.

Even while she was judging his chances, Jessie kept her eyes fixed on the horse that the outlaw was using for cover. She was not at all surprised when she saw the horse starting to move toward the cavern mouth. Even in the dimness she could see Walters's still-fettered feet shuffling between the animal's slowly plodding hooves.

Glancing over her shoulder at the triangular opening, Jessie began slowly moving toward it. She intended to be in place between Walters and his only hope of escape by the time the outlaw reached it. Once there, he would be forced to break cover in order to mount the horse he was inching toward the cave's yawning mouth now outlined against the brightening daylight.

# Chapter 14

Jessie was halfway between the mouth of the cavern and the horse shielding Walters when he peered over the animal's back and saw her moving to cut him off.

Absorbed in her effort to move silently and unseen, Jessie's attention was focused on the big cave's uneven floor. She was well aware that the outlaw could be alerted to her movements by even such a slight noise as the scraping of a bootsole across one of the rock outcrops which studded the cavern's bottom in unexpected places. Without any way of concealing herself, she would be an easy target.

At the time when Walters had first seen her, Jessie was almost certain that she'd succeed in beating him to the cave mouth and blocking his exit. Her second look told her that if Walters was given a chance to swing aside and get around her, he might succeed in reaching it. Jessie did not hesitate. Although she had one foot raised to take another careful forward step and her balance was precarious at best, she aimed her Colt quickly and let off a shot at the moving man.

Jessie's movement destroyed her balance. Spending the few seconds needed for her to get Walters squarely in her sights, while her eyes were fixed on the small arc of the outlaw's head above the horse's back, the foot that Jessie had thought she was setting on the yielding earth slipped on a rock outcrop that had been hidden by a thin film of soil. The small movement she made when shifting to aim sent the foot sliding, and her shot went wild. The bullet from her Colt screeched as it ricocheted along the far wall of the cave.

Walters fired as Jessie began to topple, but her fall saved her from the slug he'd loosed. The hot lead whistled past her head and glanced off the cavern's wall behind her. Jessie did her best to save herself from falling, but her effort had come too late. She landed on the rough stone floor in an ungainly sprawl.

Recovering quickly, Jessie began rolling across the floor to the protecting gloom of the deep shadows along the wall. She tried to keep her eyes on Walters, and when she stopped moving she discovered that in her new prone position Walters's feet and the calves of his moving legs were visible below the belly of the slowly plodding animal.

When Jessie saw the target Walters's legs offered, she swung her Colt and triggered off another fast snapshot. The bullet flew true, but now it was the movement of the horse's legs that thwarted her effort. One of the animal's hind legs was advancing as Jessie fired, and the slug hit the animal's hock squarely. Its legbone cracked almost as loudly as had the report of her pistol.

This was not the first time Jessie had heard the eerie snorting and high-pitched whinnying of a badly wounded horse. When the whistling slug from her Colt was followed by the snapping bone, the animal's scream of pain was almost like that from a human throat, but it was deeper in pitch and three times as loud. For a moment the horse stopped moving. It lifted its wounded leg and tried unsuccessfully to limp forward on three legs. Then it swayed and its hind-quarters began drooping.

Lurching sidewise, the wounded creature made a valiant effort to regain its balance. As it started to swing around, its sudden move caught Walters by surprise. He did not see the horse's rump arcing toward him until too late. When the big animal's wounded leg crumpled with its movement, the horse's rump hit Walters. He was swept off his feet by the collision and tumbled to the floor.

"Stop right where you are!" Jessie called as she swung her Colt to cover him.

Even before Jessie's command and without trying to remove the short length of rope that still stretched between his ankles, Walters had resumed his move toward the mouth of the cavern. He was crawfishing away from the fallen horse, moving as swiftly as he could with the short rope connecting his ankles and restricting their movement when he saw her raise her revolver.

Before Jessie could swing the Colt to get him in her sights, he brought down the muzzle of his own weapon and triggered off a shot. The slug whistled past Jessie's head, missing her by inches.

Jessie had already started to roll aside when she

found herself looking down the muzzle of Walters's pistol. She held her fire while rolling twice to put the prone body of the threshing horse between herself and Walters. Safely shielded behind the fallen animal, Jessie raised her head cautiously. She saw no sign of Walters. Except for herself and the prone kicking horse, the cave was empty.

Ki and Helena were making slow and not really steady progress up the canyon. The trail left by their horses along its winding muddy bottom was like a series of *v*'s and *k*'s broken by numberless *m*'s and *n*'s and *w*'s with a few *z*'s thrown in for good measure. The straggling hoofprints marked the spots where they had been forced to zigzag around puddles which Ki judged too risky to splash through because it was impossible to guess their depth or the condition of their bottoms.

Along the canyon wall the dark wet soil was broken by the bulging shapes of huge boulders as well as lesser stones only as large as a man's head protruding from the dark earth. Occasionally while they were riding through narrow stretches with steep walls, one of the big chunks of stone would pull free from its bed and tumble without warning to the canyon's soggy floor.

Small rocks, those no bigger than a man's fist or head, would throw up a small harmless but annoying splash of muddy water. Larger boulders, some the size of half a horse, landed with an impact that sent high sheets of thin soupy mud and dirty water halfway across the canyon floor. If Ki or Helena was near the spot where such monster stones happened to fall, there was no way to avoid the far-flung drops. Their faces and their clothing as well as the coats of their horses were mud-soaked and dripping by the time they'd covered a very few miles.

"I ain't sure we're smart to push ahead, the way them stones're tumbling," Helena said after they'd covered the first two or three miles. "If a great big one of 'em was to land square on us, neither us nor the nags would be fit for anything but buzzard bait."

"I'm as well aware of that as you are," Ki replied. "If it is intended that we die in such a fashion, there is no way we can avoid being hit. If we are destined to live, all the large stones will miss us."

"Maybe so, maybe no," she told him. "But I'd liefer stay alive as to die in a mess of mud."

"At least the rain's stopped," Ki said. "And we've been making good progress, considering the mud."

"I guess," she said. "But we still haven't run into Harry and the Starbuck woman. You sure you were following the right tracks?"

"I'm sure. The hoofprints along the canyon floor were very clear until the storm broke, and if there's any place along the way where they could've stopped for shelter, I certainly didn't see it."

"Far as I know, there's not anyplace up ahead where they'd've been likely to stop," Helena said with a frown. "But I never did ride up with Harry when he was doing all his scouting around. He's a close-mouthed bastard, though. When he's on a job, he don't even talk to me about what he's figuring to do."

Ki nodded, then said, "All we can do is push ahead. If they're in the canyon, we'll run into them."

Silent now, the bright sun warming their backs and casting their shadows far in front of them, they plodded ahead over the slick treacherous mud of the canyon floor.

Jessie scanned the cave mouth but saw no sign of motion. She stood up. Ignoring the pitiful whinnying of the wounded horse, she made her way carefully toward the opening. A half-dozen paces before she reached the high triangle of brightness, she angled to one side. Pressing herself to the cool slanting granite, she covered the short distance to the mouth.

Reminding herself that she had only three unfired cartridges in the Colt's cylinder and that she must make each of them count, Jessie peered cautiously around its edge. There was no sign of Walters in the limited area she could see from her concealed position. Then she stepped into the open area and saw the outlaw.

Walters was halfway across the canyon floor, plowing his way through a huge puddle of the watery mud that spanned the canyon's floor. He was almost knee-deep in the soft muck, his arms outstretched and waving to help him keep his balance on the treacherous footing. Then he raised his arms to avoid slipping, and now Jessie saw that the outlaw was clutching his pistol in his right hand and had his eyes fixed on the steep slope of the opposite wall.

Glancing across the puddled floor ahead of the fleeing outlaw, Jessie examined the face of the rise ahead of him. It was steep, but not too steep for a desperate man to climb. Huge boulders exposed by the drenching rain stuck out of the almost-vertical slant, offering footholds and handholds that would make its ascent possible.

For a moment Jessie was tempted to shoot without warning; her limited supply of shells made caution necessary. At the same time that Jessie's mind registered the need for caution, the stern but unwritten code of the West was passing subconsciously through her brain. Its dictate that even the worst outlaw should be given a fighting chance made the thought of backshooting her enemy repugnant.

"Walters!" Jessie called. "Without cover down there you haven't got a chance! Drop your gun and give up!"

As she'd expected, Walters twisted around to look back. He was raising his gun hand as he turned. When he saw Jessie in the cavern mouth, he yelled, "Go to hell and give the Devil my regards! I ain't giving up! You'll have to catch me, if you can, or shoot me if you can't!"

Jessie was raising the muzzle of her Colt when Walters fired. He shot from the hip without seeming to aim, and even though Jessie had not yet corrected her aim, she triggered off her replying shot so quickly that the two reports blended into a single burst that sounded like a small cannon had been let off and was reverberating through the canyon. The instant Jessie saw that her shot had missed, she started to step back into the cavern's protection.

Her move was a split-second too late for Jessie to escape unscathed from her exposed position. Though the slug from the outlaw's gun missed her, it screeched along the sloping archway for several inches before its velocity was spent. The bullet's impact shattered the stone only inches from Jessie's head while she was facing the high soaring arch and sent a shower of tiny stone particles into her exposed face. With the reverberations of the shots still echoing in the canyon and before Walters could fire again, Jessie completed the backward step that returned her to the protection of the high granite arch of the cave's opening.

While dodging back to regain her safe position, Jessie had closed her eyes instinctively. Only three or four of the tiny granite particles had been driven onto her eyeballs, but her eyelids had taken the brunt of the stinging shower. After she'd pulled her head behind the edge of the cave mouth, Jessie tried to open her eyes, but she had not counted on the stinging bombardment of needle-sharp, razor-edged flecks of granite that the slug from Walters's gun had sent peppering on her eyelids. When she moved her eyelids and tried to open her eyes, the tiny granite shards rasped on her eyeballs and eyelids alike.

Jessie's eyes began watering profusely and the shimmering veil of tears soon ended the pain, but though she was able to part her eyelids in tiny slits and could see the edge of the cave mouth as a distorted and wavy shimmering shadow, this vestige of vision did not help her a great deal.

Blinking, Jessie dashed the tears away with the back of her hand before peering around the edge of the opening again. Through the dancing, wavering blurred distance that separated her from the fleeing outlaw, she could only sense rather than see that Walters was moving again. The flicks of her eyelids were clearing Jessie's vision, but she realized that with only two live shells remaining in her Colt, she could take no chances. She pulled her head back quickly and continued to blink rapidly while she waited for her eyes to return to normal.

"Those were shots!" Ki exclaimed. "And they weren't very far ahead of us!"

"That's right," Helena agreed. "And we don't have to ask who's doing the shooting. There's not likely to be anybody but Harry and that lady boss of yours in this part of the canyon so soon after the kind of rain we just had."

"We've got to move faster!" Ki went on, digging his heels into the sides of his mount and slapping the reins on its neck. "If Jessie's in trouble—"

Helena broke in to say, "Harry's got a way of carrying a load of trouble with him. But we won't get these nags to make any better time, not in this muck we're fighting."

Ki had made his decision while Helena was speaking. He leaned toward her and handed her the reins of his horse as he said, "That shooting wasn't very far away. I can climb up on the canyon wall and make better time on foot. Here. You lead my horse and come ahead."

"You figure you can trust me?"

"I think I have to," Ki replied. "But if you try to get away—"

"You and the Starbuck woman will come after me," Helena broke in. "If you get the better of Harry."

Her last words fell into the empty air, for Ki was already a dozen yards away. He was running at top speed in a long slant that would allow him to move faster and make better forward progress than a straight upward climb. She watched him until his progress took him into a section of the wall where it curved out of sight.

Ki had not looked back at Helena. He had eyes for nothing except the steeply sloping stretch of canyon wall ahead of him. With every forward step he was choosing the direction to take in the next few yards of his progress. Like the opposite wall, the one he was traversing not only slanted sharply, but was studded with the protruding bulges of boulders that varied from head-sized to those as large as a small shanty.

Even with all the detours he was forced to make around the rocks too large to jump across, Ki moved fast. He chose no special course, but adapted his path as was needed to make the best possible forward progress while avoiding the boulders he could not easily step or jump over. Now and then one of his feet landed in a soft spot or a puddled dent where rainwater had filled a hole left by a fallen boulder.

Ahead of him, Ki saw the canyon's curved course beginning to straighten out. By the time he rounded the curvature and had a clear view along both walls of the canyon, the last echoes of the shots exchanged between Jessie and Walters had faded into silence. There was no sign of Jessie, but he saw Walters struggling through the deep heavily clinging mud.

When Ki scanned the limited landscape again, looking for Jessie, he discovered the mouth of the cavern. He realized at once that while riding through the canyon the night before, he had passed the cave without seeing it in the rain and darkness, but the realization gave him no comfort. He returned his attention to Walters. By this time the outlaw had reached the opposite wall of the canyon and was beginning to climb up it.

A quick scanning look was enough to tell Ki that he was still much too far away from Walters to reach him by throwing a *shuriken* from the case strapped to his forearm. He had no other weapon, so he concentrated on picking his way along the slanting canyon wall to find a place where he could cross quickly and climb the canyon's opposite wall at a slant to intercept Walters and keep him from escaping.

By the time Ki had found a place that promised a

quick ascent to the canyon's rim, Walters had finished crossing the mucky canyon floor and was beginning to zigzag his way up the steeply slanting wall. The place he'd chosen for his ascent was twenty or thirty yards up the canyon from the mouth of the cave, and as Ki began his own effort to cross Jessie stepped out of the black forbidding opening.

She did not see Ki; her eyes were fixed on Walters, who was moving steadily upward toward the canyon rim in spite of the erratic zigzag course he was forced to follow. Jessie had stopped outside the cave mouth and was raising her Colt until Ki's shout stopped her arm in midair.

"Jessie!" he called. "Don't shoot! A bullet's too quick and easy! Let's take him alive and see that he goes to prison!"

"Ki!" Jessie replied. "Where did you come from?"

"It'd take too long to tell you!" Ki called back. "We'll take Walters first, then we can have a talk and sort everything out!"

"Go ahead, then," Jessie agreed. "Remember, he's got a gun, but he's not in a position to do any accurate shooting. Besides, I don't think he has more than one or two cartridges left in it!"

Ki began picking his way across the soft rain-puddled mud that the bottom of the canyon had become after the rain. He knew from their past scrapes with danger that Jessie could take care of herself and knew that they'd faced so many similar situations, she would make quick correct decisions.

After watching Ki for a few moments and seeing him moving fairly easily in spite of the mucky footing, Jessie returned her attention to Walters. He had reached the canyon's opposite wall now and was beginning to mount its side. His progress was not easy, and Jessie raised her Colt. When she tried to get him clearly in its sights, the blurring of her eyes after their shower of granite dust kept her from taking the precise aim that was needed for accurate shooting at such a distance.

Reluctantly, Jessie released the pressure of her trigger finger. With only two rounds remaining in the Colt's cylinder, she could not afford a miss, for she was now acting as a backup for Ki. She kept her revolver covering Walters, but turned her eyes to look at Ki. He was making only a little better progress than the outlaw had in his efforts to scale the steep rock-studded canyon wall. Glancing quickly across her revolver's sights and adjusting her aim again, Jessie waited.

Across the yawning canyon, Ki was now beginning to make his way up the wall's steep slope. The mud was almost as slick as that on the floor of the canyon, but his superb physical condition and skill enabled him to move faster than had Walters. As he climbed, Ki glanced upward not only to pick the best course to follow, but to keep an eye on Walters's movements. The outlaw was still beyond the range of Ki's *shuriken*, but Walters had paused several times, picking the best course to follow, while Ki's greater muscular skill and lighter weight enabled him to move faster.

Walters had paused momentarily. His head was tilted far back as he searched the upslope, trying to pick the easiest path. He'd stopped at the bottom of a huge boulder, almost the size of a modest house, which protruded from the canyon wall. The outlaw was moving his head from side to side, craning his neck as he attempted to see what lay beyond the

179

massive chunk of rock that was blocking his path. After he'd failed in his effort, Walters began moving again, sidling horizontally across the face of the high bluff to make a detour around the boulder.

★

# Chapter 15

Ki had continued to move steadily and a quick glance upslope told him that he was now almost close enough to Walters for a *shuriken* to be effective. He'd paused only once, and then only long enough to slip one of the razor-edged throwing blades from the leather carrying case strapped to his forearm. Moving his hand with care, he slid the throwing blade into his mouth and gripped it between his jaws, then resumed his climb. He tried to move faster, to get within range of the outlaw before Walters could climb around the huge rock and put it between them.

Glancing up at Walters again after picking his route, Ki saw that the renegade was indeed attempting to move around the massive boulder and keep it as a shield between them. He saw a narrow rock outcrop ahead and pushed hard to reach it before Walters got beyond his throwing range.

Giving almost as much attention to Ki as he did to finding fresh toeholds, Walters tried to move faster. He was scrabbling across the strip of wet earth below the boulder when the massive hunk of stone shifted a few inches. Ki saw the rock move a hands-breadth and saw Walters scrabbling wildly as the outlaw tried to put on a burst of speed in an effort to get beyond it.

His efforts were too little and too late. As small as the boulder's move had been, it shifted the big stone's center of gravity, and once the movement of the massive rock had started, there was no counter-force that could stop it.

Slowly but inexorably the boulder continued to tilt and the thin rain-soaked dirt below it started slipping in a wide strip down the steep face of the canyon's wall. Walters's feet began churning faster as he felt the earth moving beneath them. His effort to escape may have contributed to his doom. The boulder continued to slip, and the trickle of muddy soil became a streamlike flow as it slid down the steep incline.

Walters was visible for only a few moments. The soft wet soil engulfed him quickly, and the last sight that either Jessie or Ki got of the outlaw was his flailing feet. Then the strip of wet earth beneath the boulder began flowing like a river as the huge rock gained speed and pushed on down the long slant until it thudded to a halt on the floor of the canyon.

Jessie had watched the big boulder's downward course from the moment it started. Ki had seen it from his precarious perch on the canyon wall. Neither of them spoke for several moments after the boulder came to rest atop the pile of earth that had grown head-high within the few minutes required for the earthslide to come to an end.

"You're all right, aren't you, Ki?" Jessie called when she saw Ki starting to descend the canyon wall.

"Of course," he replied. "I'll be with you in a

minute. Right now I'm just being thankful that I didn't manage to get any closer to Walters before that slide began."

"I don't suppose there's any chance he'd still be alive?" Jessie asked as she watched Ki's fast nimble progress to the canyon floor.

"Of course not. Even if we had a crew of diggers with the shovels they'd need, we couldn't uncover him in time to get him out alive."

"Then we don't have to stay here any longer, and the faster we start home the happier I'll be."

Ki thought of Helena and replied, "I ran into Walters's woman while I was looking for you. She was supposed to follow me, but I have a hunch she'd gotten close enough to see what happened and is well on her way in the other direction by now. And I left my horse with her."

Jessie did not reply for a moment, then she said, "We've got another thief to deal with in Silver City, Ki. And there's the market herd to handle. Now, there's a horse in the cave over there. It belonged to Walters. Let's call taking it a trade and go home. I didn't come here of my own free will in the first place, and I don't want to stay here any longer, so close to that renegade ranger's grave."

Watch for

**LONE STAR AND THE RIPPER**

93rd novel in the exciting LONE STAR series
from Jove

*Coming in May!*

# From the Creators of Longarm!

Featuring the beautiful Jessica Starbuck
and her loyal half-American half-
Japanese martial arts sidekick Ki.